BLACK
SCORPION

NOVEL

DR MUSTAFA ROSTOM

www.newgeneration-publishing.com

 **New Generation Publishing**

CHAPTER ONE

Today was a special celebration for the Abrucci family. This Italian upper class, business-oriented family lived in a sophisticated, very lavish estate, a block away from the Beverly Hills Motel in California. Relatives and friends had filled the spacious vacuum of the estate to honour the marriage of Dina, the second youngest member of the Abrucci family. All the preparations for the home wedding that afternoon had not quite yet settled in their right place, but for Sylvana, the mother of three boys and her only daughter, Dina, there was still sometime before there may be any need for panic. But all the same, Sylvana felt restless and very nervous. She made her way through dispersed, yet clustered small groups of guests, and towards her husband.

Her husband Dominic stood at the front door, in a black tuxedo, welcoming new guests. By then Sylvana had approached him, both exchanging warm smiles. She had greeted the last man passing through the doorway, and turned to fix the bright red rose that seemed to be loosely pinned to her husband's tuxedo. Dominic was 14 years her senior, with grey wavy hair centred around his bold hairline.

'How's it all going sweetheart?' Sylvana asked, using her index finger to sort the floral surrounding the rose.

'Okay, darling! Everything's okay with the kids?' Dominic responded.

'Well, we're still waiting for Tony to finalize some business papers at the company, and Joe called earlier to see if we needed anything, as he was just about to leave the restaurant', she smiled.

'What about the bride and groom?'

'Dina is upstairs getting her tiara and make-up sorted, and your brother-in-law Nunzio is also finalizing some company documents, before leaving with Tony to come home.'

It seemed that Dominic was beginning to feel a little nervous, after glancing at the huge sterling silver Geneva wall clock in the hallway, which read one p.m. Dominic and Sylvana knew that the wedding celebrant was to arrive in two hours.

'What about our little bambino, Gino?' Dominic asked, grabbing a hold of both Sylvana's hands. Gino was their youngest son, although he was hardly a baby at fourteen. But to Dominic and Sylvana he would always be the baby of the family, and the precious last one.

'Gino is also upstairs getting into his tuxedo'. Sylvana informed him, giving him a soft pinch on the cheek. She could see some of her husband's business colleagues greeting each other, as they headed towards the front door. 'I'll run up and check on Dina and Gino. Don't worry the boys shall be home soon', Sylvana reassured him. He sighed as she let go of his hands and headed off towards the staircase.

She went upstairs to Dina's room where she found two beauticians polishing her face with extra foundation and setting her fake hand nails one by one. Dina's friends were her brides mates, who stood beside her in crimson satin floral gowns with a streak of tiny white daisies pinned across the top of their heads. They seemed to be giggling, holding firm onto their champagne goblets. Sylvana leaned against the doorway, consumed with tears, and overwhelmed with joy. Dina had reminded her of her wedding day. How she was surrounded by close friends. Besides Dina was somewhat a spitting image of her mother. They both shared big brown eyes, an olive complexion, and dead straight long black hair. Although Sylvana's hair today did not reach her waistline, she had it up in a French

4

fox with streaks of greyness in it. At fifty three years of age, grey hairs were to be expected.

'Hi! Mama', Dina yelled from across the room, 'Come in', she said, waving her arm, before promptly returning it to the beautician.

'Oh! You look very beautiful. Bellissimo. Like a true princess.' She leaned forward to hug Dina.

'Oh! Mama, just be happy. Don't cry you'll ruin our make-up.' Dina exclaimed with a broad grin.

'You have grown up so quickly, my darling. I wasn't expecting to see you as a bride so soon.'

'I'm twenty six years old, and it was only two years ago since my graduation. It was only soon that marriage was to be expected. Papa and you had always wanted me to marry after completing my studies.' Dina smiled, and Sylvana was still consumed with tears which she could hardly hold in, as her lips shivered. She was very elated by the wedding celebration that was going to take place today of her only daughter.

Dina had graduated two years ago with a psychology degree from the University of California, but was strongly influenced by her parents' conservative ideals of females being nurturers, despite their academic merits. Besides Dina did not care too much to express a progressive view on this issue. She was used to growing up in an Italian cultural atmosphere, where both her parents and relatives had maintained and strongly expressed ethnic family values. 'And he's Italian', Dina was quick to point out, referring to her husband to be. She knew her parents were against the idea of intra-marriage, and had always wished for their children to marry spouses of a similar cultural background. They both smiled, and one of Dina's brides mate suggested that she wears her girdle.

'I'll see how Gino is doing, before I get back to things downstairs', Sylvana said, and left the room.

Meanwhile, Tony stood firm beside his fax machine with a briefcase in one hand and a collection of memorandums in the other. He was reading his last memo, before leaving his office. He was thirty four years old, and the eldest sibling in the Abrucci family. Tony was his father's favourite son, and as a result had to live with the burden of his brothers' jealousy for years. He had graduated with a degree in business and finance, and had worked in the family's pasta company for the past ten years. He still holds the position of co-executive manager in the company, and constantly receives the blessings of his father. Dominic adores Tony immensely, because unlike his brother Joe, he has proved to be a worthy family and business-orientated gentleman.

'Are we ready to leave?' his brother-in-law to be spoke, as he popped his head through the office door. Tony nodded, and threw him his car keys.

'Start her up. I'll be down in two secs. I'm just going to give Consuela a call'.

Tony was married to Consuela from Italy, and has a young son, named Fabio. Fabio was born on Valentine's Day and Consuela thought the name was appropriate, as he was handsome, and she thought he was going to break the hearts of many girls when he was older.

Tony was always immersed with the business, and had left all family issues in the hands of Consuela. Consuela was a very neurotic person, and tended to shed erratic and very strange behaviours at times. They didn't share much of a loving marital life. She enjoyed spending Tony's money on shopping sprees and outings with her Italian girlfriends.

'Hello. Hello. Consuela. It's me Tony. I'm just about to head to my parents. How are you going time wise.' He asked.

'I'm just about to arrive at your parent's estate. I'll see you there.'

'Okay! Bye.' He hung up.

Back at the Abrucci estate, Sylvana knocked on Gino's door.

'Gino. May I come in darling', and she let herself in. Gino was chatting on the internet and felt very awkward as he quickly shut down his computer to a screen saver mode. He was always annoyed by his mother's unexpected intrudence. He felt she never gave him sufficient warning before entering his room, and he interpreted such action as invasion of privacy.

'How many times have I told you not to do that?' He raised his voice. Sylvana could see he was frantic about covering something from her, but she never queried his behaviour, because he had been doing this for the past two months. She just dismissed his behaviour as being nothing serious, but that her son did not want her to pry on his cyber conversations.

'Just seeing how you were doing baby', his mother quietly remarked. She also did not question his tone of voice, because of his physical disability. Gino was a fourteen year old quadriplegic bound to a wheelchair for life. He sustained major injuries to his lower spine after being involved in a car accident with his parents, five years ago. He blamed his father for the accident, because Dominic and Sylvana had argued about Dominic not wanting to go that night to the wedding of Sonia's daughter. Sonia was Sylvana's best friend, and they had grown up together as youngsters back in Rome.

Gino continued to have nightmares about that particular night, and at times would wake up in the middle of the night in a pool of sweat. He distinctly remembers his father drinking a whole bottle of Burgundy and Rum out on the front patio, while his mother was upstairs wearing her night gown. And by the time they had got in the car, Gino had noticed that his father was heavily consumed with alcohol. His mother could smell the stench of alcohol, but was desperate on not missing the wedding, and had made the choice to risk a ride with Dominic. She had never learnt to drive a motor vehicle, and wanted Dominic desperately beside her at the wedding function. At that time she couldn't call a taxi, because her electricity had been down, and she was running very late.

Gino vividly remembers his parents being very upset and had continued to argue inside the car. He remembers feeling very scared sitting in the back, and his mother at times shouting at Dominic to slow down. Later, he recalls a huge beam of white light coming through the front screen, and shattered glass particles flying towards him. That was all he could remember, and later some of the cold operating instruments that were initially used by doctors in theatre.

Gino mainly blamed his father for drink driving, and somewhat his mother for taking the risk of accompanying him in the vehicle. But all the feelings of remorse and guilt that both Dominic and Sylvana had felt, including Gino's feelings of rage and despise towards them, mainly Dominic, had been left buried deep inside of them. Dominic had refused back then to participate in family group therapy. He didn't believe in psychoanalysis, and felt that this stuff was just for quacks. He believed that it was up to the individual to resolve his or her feelings on their own, even if it took many years to do so.

'Mama! I'll be right in fitting into my tux. Besides I can dress myself you know.' Gino stated. He didn't like to talk much with his parents, and preferred to get to the point quickly.

'Well! You better hurry up darling. Your brothers

are expected to arrive soon.' She gave him a soft kiss on the forehead, and smiled as she backed away from him. Gino responded with a slight grin, and she left.

Tony and his brother-in-law to be, Nunzio, were making their way down the L.A. highway and towards the estate. The wind gushed through their hair, as they sat firmly in Tony's blue Corvette.

'Can't you make this precious metal thing go any faster', Nunzio suggested, and Tony slightly glanced towards him.

'Relax, there's still an hour and forty minutes to go. We have only forty minutes to get home. You want to get married in one piece, don't you?' Tony smiled as he looked ahead of him. Nunzio just shook his head with a smile, and took off his sunglasses. 'Are you nervous?' Tony asked amidst the sound of the motor and the strong winds.

'Not really! Just a little', Nunzio replied.

There was no need for Nunzio to be too nervous, he had become a close companion of the family, ever since he began working as a business associate with the family's company six months ago. Tony had liked his work for the company, and his father Dominic, thought very highly of Nunzio. Dominic felt Nunzio had true Sicilian blood and was a commendable businessman. Dominic had allowed Nunzio to enter into his heart, and had shared great loyalty, trust and true friendship with him. He had constantly invited Nunzio for family dinners in the past two months. And he could envisage him as the long lost, perfect Italian groom for his only daughter, Dina.

Dominic felt that Dina was a good and gentle, educated girl, and that she had equally deserved a good and well educated Italian husband. Dominic had spontaneously suggested the idea of marriage between Dina and Nunzio, a month ago, over a family dinner, and to his surprise the family did not challenge the idea. Nunzio had fitted well into the Abrucci family, especially in the past two months. He had managed to gain the confidence and liking of all members. For many members of the Abrucci family, Nunzio was an easy person to talk to, and they all had felt comfortable in sharing their intimate feelings with him. He was the ideal Samaritan to the family, and he was especially a Saint in the eyes of Gino.

'Hey! I guess this is the last chance, and I guess the appropriate time to tell you, that you better take good care of my kid sister. I hope you will provide her with the warmth and love that all the Abrucci's are used to.' Tony smiled at Nunzio.

'Dina is my heart. She is my whole life. So don't worry, Dina will receive the best love and affection that any decent Italian girl deserves. And more.' And on that note they both were stunned by the loud bust that seemed to come from the back of the car.

'What's that noise?' Nunzio said, with wide open eyes, as he looked towards Tony. By then Tony was experiencing some difficulty in controlling the steering wheel, and had pulled over to the side of the road just at the end of the highway.

'I don't know. But my guess is one of the back tyres has had it.'

'Oh! No. We're going to be late to the wedding.' Nunzio looked worried as he said it. And Tony had just got out to inspect the back wheel. He could see that the tyre's valve had been severely ruptured, and that he needed to use the spare wheel.

'Don't panic, I'll fix it quickly. Just chuck us the keys.'

Nunzio came out of the vehicle with the keys, and Tony gave him his tuxedo jacket. Tony and Nunzio had earlier worn their tuxedos in their final work hour.

They thought they may not have time to change later at the estate.

'Help me with the jack, and roll out that blanket for me. I don't want my tux to get dirty.' Tony told Nunzio.

It had taken Tony the next twenty minutes to add the spare wheel onto the car. His mother had called Tony on his mobile to see what was taking them so long. He explained to her about the flat tyre, and had reassured her that everything was fine, and that they'll be home in the next twenty minutes or so.

Back at the Abrucci estate, Sylvana had called her son Joe to also inquire about his absence.

'Hello! Joe. Where are you? What's taking you so long? Haven't you finished fixing your paper work at the restaurant?'

'Yes Mama, I'm on my way home. I had to see the accountant about some business papers. Ciao!'

Joe was their second eldest son, and he never continued with tertiary studies, and had never lived up to his father's expectations. He shared a closer bond with his mother. And he had always gone through life as a social delinquent and a wicked rebel. In the eyes of his father, Joe was the black sheep in the family. Dominic felt that his son Joe was easily influenced by the hooligans and villains that he befriended outside the family. Dominic had many times in the past wished to disown him as a son. But Dominic had to respect the wishes of his wife, Sylvana. There was no way she would allow Dominic to castrate Joe from the family. Joe was part of her soul, her heart, her blood and veins. She had given birth to him, and felt that her son was a piece of her body. She was certainly not willing to dismiss Joe, nor her feelings of unconditional love towards him at the expense of Dominic. In the past years, Dominic had learnt to tolerate Joe's misdemeanors with great difficulty. He knew that he would have to lose Sylvana, if he was to castrate his mischievous son from the Abrucci family. It was Sylvana who had in the past year convinced Dominic to give Joe the family's Italian restaurant in Bel Air. Dominic was also not so sure he had made the right decision in delegating such an important family business to Joe. But he mainly did it for Sylvana's sake. He loved her dearly and wanted her to be always happy.

Sylvana had hung up the phone after having spoken to her son Joe. She noticed that there was thirty five minutes until the ceremony commenced, and let out a great sigh. She had hoped that her sons would come back home in time. Her best friend Sonia had called out to her from behind one of the ushers holding a tray of wine goblets. 'Ya hoo! Sylvana darling.' She grabbed a wine goblet from the usher, smiled to him, and came closer to Sylvana, giving her a great big kiss on the cheek. 'What's the matter honey? You seem a little edgy.'

'I'm a little edgy, because my sons are yet to arrive. I mean they called, thank Christ, but I hope they come soon. This is a very special day for Dina, and I don't want anything to go wrong', she exclaimed with an expression of despair.

'Don't worry my darling I'm sure they're on their way.' Sonia reassured her, rubbing Sylvana's shoulders. 'Oh! Here comes your not so perfect daughter-in-law. Oh! Well..Ciao darling.' Sonia said, took her last gulp of wine, and left.

Sylvana could see Consuela and her son Fabio walking across the garden, dodging caterers with large silver trays filled with all sorts of Italian cuisine, including Dina's favourite Lasagna. Consuela had finally made her way up to Sylvana. And they both greeted each other with hugs and kisses. And Sylvana lifted up Fabio into her arms, slobbering him with affectionate kisses. He was her first grandchild, and she was anticipating Dina's child next. Sylvana did not think much of Consuela, but she pretended to like her for Tony's sake. Both Dominic and Sylvana felt that Tony could have found himself a better Italian wife than Consuela. But overall they had learned to keep their distance from Tony's marital life, and did not wish to create havoc in Tony's life. They just wanted Tony to be happy. Dominic and Sylvana had always quietly confided in each other about some of Consuela's inappropriate behaviours.

'I'll go and check on how Dina is doing. Why don't you mingle with the crowd.' Sylvana said, passing Fabio into Consuela's arms.

Sylvana walked down an aisle of floral bouquets, mainly enriched with white and purple Jasmins. She made her way through the back patio, greeting guests, as she headed to the staircase. She realized that Dina was just about to come down. 'Everything okay sweetheart?'

'Yes Mama. I'm just worried about Tony, Joe and Nunzio not making it on time.' And soon as she had completed her words, Dina noticed that Joe had appeared behind her mother. He had also been wearing his black tux, and Sylvana greeted him with an affectionate kiss.

'Have you seen your brother Tony?' Sylvana asked, as she gently caressed Joe's cheek.

'Yes Mama. He's just using one of the garages to park his car. And Nunzio is with him too.'

The marriage celebrant had just arrived on time, and Tony and Nunzio came dashing through the front door right behind him. Dina slightly squealed and rushed two steps back, to avoid being seen by the groom prior

13

to the wedding ceremony. Sylvana told Joe and Nunzio to escort Father Vincent to Dominic, and suggested to Tony to use their bathroom to clear the spot of oil grease on his chin. 'And check up on Gino, and ask him to come down please.' Sylvana shouted out to Tony as he headed midway up the staircase.

Moments later, guests were seated in the estate garden in rows with huge floral setting and bow tie ribbons at the edge of each aisle. All guests seemed well groomed and dressed, and Father Vincent stood under a white floral arch with colossal tied ribbons on both sides. To the left side of Father Vincent the musician began to play the org, and to his left stood Nunzio and Tony with the rings as his best man. On the outskirts of the guests stood a number of white round tables, each table having its own floral bouquet placed in the middle of it. Nunzio and Tony smiled at each other as they saw Sylvana and Joe making their way down the aisle and to the right side of the wedding celebrant. They were then followed by Consuela, Fabio and Gino, and after them came Dominic and Dina at a slower pace. Dina felt very nervous and was glad to cling onto her father. She looked quite dashing and radiant in her bridal gown. Her gown was partly satin and her low-cut back vest was pierced with many pieces of crystals, pearls, diamond studs and zirconia. She wore a simple diamond tiara, which held her fringe back, allowing her twirled pieces of black hair to dangle down the back of her neck.

She held a floral bouquet of white Jasmine, as they were her favourites, smiling to guests as she slowly paced down the aisle. Dominic and Dina were also slowly followed by three bride mates, throwing tiny white daisies behind them. Dina was impressed by the trouble her father had gone through to provide her with an extravagant wedding that looked like one out of a

Hollywood movie. She was mainly impressed by the tiny yellow pebble lights that decorated all the palm trees on the outskirts of the estate.

Dominic placed Dina's hands into Nunzio's and squeezed them tight, before stepping back, exchanging a distinguished look with Nunzio as he did it. Throughout the ceremony, Sylvana could not control her quiet sobs as Nunzio and Dina exchanged wedding vows, cut the cake, released the girdle, waltzed in the garden among guests, exchanged drinks, as well as relatives and friends burying Dina with gold jewelery. Dominic approached the happy couple, with Sylvana by his side, and also provided his best wishes, while placing an expensive Rolex gold watch onto Nunzio's wrist.

'Thank you! Dominic, you shouldn't have troubled yourself.' Nunzio said, hugging him.

'Oh! Not much trouble. You're like a son to me now', Dominic spoke, suppressing a tear in his eye. And both Dina and her mother were once again consumed with tears, touched by Dominic's warmth and affection. The D.J. began to play Italian music, and both Dominic and Sylvana were taken in by the grand circle some of the guests had made, while Nunzio and Dina laughed and began to cheer and clap as they sat back into the seats on the other side of the table.

The sun was starting to set among the estate, and with the extra bright lights that dimmed across the trees and garden gazebos, the wedding had even looked extra sensational. By then the music had gone a little quieter, and some of the guests had already left, leaving only a handful scattered across the estate garden. From one side, beside the beverage table, stood Dominic and Sylvana each holding Chardonnay goblets.

'The wedding has been a great success, and I am so happy. I am very happy that Dina's special day has gone so well. And it's great to see her always smiling and very happy.' Sylvana commented, slightly leaning her head onto Dominic. Dominic hugged her around the waistline.

'Well! Senorita. I couldn't agree more', whincing his eyes with a great big grin. 'You have a beautiful daughter. She is just like her mother.' Dominic informed her, as he gently rubbed his cheek onto hers. They both stood silently across the garden, gazing at Nunzio and Dina exchanging smiles and words with their three sons, and two of Nunzio's business colleagues.

One of the estate's maids was making her way towards Dominic with a packaged box; she had earlier discovered on the front patio.

'Sir, I have found this strange parcel outside the front door, earlier this evening.' The maid informed him reaching out hers arms with the box towards him.

'Are you sure it's for me?' Dominic asked, looking very intrigued and puzzled by the white box with a black ribbon tied to it.

'Yes sir. It has your name on it.' The maid said, and left. Dominic looked bewildered and a little stunned, holding the box in his hands.

'Well! Open it, and see what's inside it.' Sylvana also looked a little stunned, and was curious to know what was inside it.

When Dominic began to open the box, he could tell it was going to take a bit of effort, as the inner package of the box was engulfed with tightly taped styrofoam. After breaking through the initial exterior, a bad stench was released from inside the box, and both Dominic and Sylvana had noticed the thilthy aroma.

'What's that smell?' Sylvana asked pinching her nose.

'I don't know. But this better not be a sick joke

initiated by some workers at the company', Dominic answered. It had already seemed like they were about to discover an unexpected thing, and Dominic was not amused by what he was suspecting to be some sick prank. He had fired company workers in the past, but he had never experienced any form of harassment subsequent to them leaving the job. He began to feel a little sickened and terrified, as he aggressively ripped through the rest of the package.

A dead black scorpion, that was beginning to decapitate, with a small silver sword, and a black stemmed rose had fallen onto the lawn next to Sylvana's feet. Sylvana had let out a slight scream, and jumped back with great fright. She had attracted the attention of the guests that surrounded her, including her own kids. All her family and a couple of business colleagues, including Consuela came rushing up towards them. They all were quiet for a moment, looking stunned, with some faces shocked, by the three strange objects that lay on the lawn. 'Ooo'oo! Grosse', Consuela said, running off into the house with her son and her nose pinched.

'What kind of a sick joke is that?' Joe remarked.

Sylvana and Tony had noticed that Dominic was very pale and did not look so well, as he maintained to stare at the black scorpion, the strange monolithic looking silver sword, and the black rose. Dominic did not say a word, but a moment later looked up to the trivialized faces of Tony and Sylvana, and said, 'Oh! My God. Oh! My God. My past has come to haunt me.' They all felt estranged by Dominic's comment. It did not make sense what Dominic's past had to do with the things that lay on the lawn. Sylvana could see that Dominic was feeling somewhat frail and seemed a little weak. She told Tony and Joe to grab a hold of their father, and to take him up to his room. Dina grabbed a hold of Gino's wheelchair, and followed their father from behind. Nunzio remained behind staring silently at the lawn. Sylvana placed her hand on his shoulder, and stared into his eyes with despair.

'This is one sick joke. Don't worry Sylvana. I'll see to the rest of the guests.' Nunzio said.

Upstairs Dominic's sons laid him gently onto the gold jacquard bed cover. Joe had returned to the guests, and informed Dina and Gino to let their father rest. Shortly afterwards, Sylvana entered their bedroom, and found her husband asleep, and Tony staring outside the bedroom window. Tony had been the most handsome one out of the boys. He stood very tall beside the window, with pale blue eyes and fair golden hair complexion. Her best friend Sonia had always teased her about Tony's looks. She jokingly remarked that the doctors had given Sylvana the wrong child. It was not to say that all Italians could not be blondes, but Sonia was aware that there were no blondes in Sylvana's family, let alone their Italian village. Sylvana quietly walked up to Tony.

'How's your father doing?'

'He's okay Mama. Papa's just having a little rest.' Tony turned to his mother and put his hands on her shoulders. 'I wonder what Papa meant with what he said earlier down there?'

'I don't know son. But your Papa sure looked as if he'd seen a ghost downstairs. He looked terrified as he stared at those things.' Sylvana replied, as she gently pulled a large wooden crucifix from the dressing table and placed it on top of their bed. 'Your Papa's eyes. They seemed to light up with fear. I don't understand son. The memory of your father's eyes sends cold chills down my spine.' She added, as she lit three small candles on the dressing table.

'I wonder what a black scorpion, a sword and a

black rose have to do with Papa's past.' Tony sounded curious.

'I guess your Papa has all the answers.' She tiredly spoke to her son. And she had hoped Dominic would spill the beans. She knew her husband quite well, and at times he opted not to disclose his personal feelings. Dominic was a stubborn, reserved man in moments of family crises. He found it difficult to express his feelings, even to his wife. And despite the magnitude of life's hardships, Dominic did a good job of always suppressing the pain. And even when Sylvana could sense he was in a great deal of pain, Dominic always revealed a rough exterior. Sylvana felt that it was hard to understand her husband's personality, especially his emotional side.

Dina had entered the room. 'How's Papa? Mama', she sadly spoke, and knelt down next to Sylvana.

'Oh! He'll be allright, Ballerina. You're Papa is strong as an ox. After he's had a little rest, he'll be able to tell us what those things might have meant to him.' Joe walked in carrying the three odd objects on a silver tray.

'What shall I do with those, Mama?'

Tony was prompt in responding to his question. 'Why the hell did you bring those things up here?' he sounded a little annoyed, 'Didn't you realize, it was those things that got Papa very upset. Throw them in the trash can for Pete's sake.'

'No. No. Keep them. Your father may want to see them again. They may give him more ideas about his past. Put them on top of the drawer in the hallway', Sylvana informed Joe.

'All the guests have left. I'll go back down and finish helping Nunzio bring the presents inside. By the way Nunz is asking about you', Joe looked towards Dina, 'Aren't you both going to be late for the airport?'

'I don't know if we should go to Hawaii, considering what's happened with Papa?' Dina sadly said.

'No, Ballerina. Besides your father would be upset. Your brothers went through a lot of trouble preparing this honeymoon for you and Nunzio. And besides your father's just having a rest. There's nothing to worry about. Tony and I are staying right here beside him. You go my little princess. Go and have a good time. I'll fill you in on everything when you return'. Her mother reassured her.

'What about Consuela and Fabio. Don't they need you to be with them tonight?' Dina asked, looking directly ahead of her at Tony.

'Don't worry about them. Consuela came in her car, and left after Papa opened the parcel. Besides, Consuela is used to being alone whenever Papa and I went off on business trips. Anyway I need to know what Papa has to say about those ridiculous things.' Tony pointed at the tray Joe was holding.

'C'mon Sis, up you get. I'll drive you and Nunz to the airport. We better hurry there is forty minutes left until your plane's departure.' Joe said, and left. Dina thanked Sylvana and her brother, and kissed them both, before leaving the room. Sylvana turned towards Dominic and let out a great sigh, while Tony sat back in the corner chair, and let out a deep breath.

A few minutes later, Gino entered his parents' bedroom in his wheelchair. 'How's Papa, Mama?' Gino asked. Not that he cared so much about his parents, but asked out of courtesy. He blamed his parents for the car accident, and had distant himself emotionally and somewhat physically, ever since the accident five years ago. He somewhat felt a little sympathy towards his mother at times, but felt that his cold manner and apprehension towards his parents, was their fault.

'Everything is allright, my little Bambino. Papa is just having a little rest.' Sylvana replied, as she gave him a great sloppy kiss on the cheek. Gino gave her a small grin, and at the same time felt his body nerves shake. He felt very mature for his age, and besides at fourteen, he saw himself as a young man. He preferred not to be kissed by his mother like a small child, especially when she did it in front of his brothers.

'How's it going at Youth camp?' Tony asked him.

'Oh! So and so. It's okay. I like hanging around John and Matt, and sharing the cabin with them. I won a race medal the other day. Our camp coordinator thinks I'm a real champ at rowing'. He spoke with a large grin.

'Good on you champ.' Tony tapped his little brother on the shoulder. Sylvana ruffled her hands to her sons, pointing out that their father had opened his eyes, and the three of them moved closer to his beside.

'How are you feeling Papa? You had us all worried back there.' Tony said, as he squeezed his father's hand.

'I'm okay son'.

'How are you feeling, Dominic?' Sylvana also asked, as she helped him to sit up, and placed two extra pillows behind his back.

'I'm allright sweetheart.'

'Would you like me to get you some iced tea or a lemon drink?'

'No. Thank you sweetheart.' She used a handkerchief to wipe some of the sweat across his forehead.

'Papa. Can you tell us why those things in the box had upset you?' Tony asked him.

'Those things symbolize some of my past back in Italy.' He began to explain to Tony the connection between the three objects and his past. Sylvana was

21

amazed by Dominic easily opening up to something that obviously had deep meanings for him. She thought they needed to torture him to get him to speak, when he came around. Sylvana was very surprised by Dominic's lack of resistance to open up and to confide in his family. But then again, she realized that Tony was present in the room, and that he usually felt comfortable in discussing many things with him.

'When I was young, I was forced to join a large mafia group in Italy. They called themselves the Black Scorpion. My father had gambled with them and lost, and he could not repay his debt. So one night, the leader and some of his members forced themselves into our home', Dominic was finding it hard to hold back some tears, as his upper lip slightly shivered, and he kept swallowing his saliva. 'They cut some of my father's fingers off, while the rest of my family was forced to watch. Then they threatened to shoot us all, one-by-one, starting with my father', Sylvana began to rub Dominic's hand, as her eyes filled with tears. 'But before Antonio had pulled the trigger, that was the leader. Before he pulled the trigger, I cried and kissed his hand, and begged him not to kill my father.' Dominic continued to explain as a few tears trickled down his cheeks. 'I offered to be Antonio's slave, if he was to spare my father's life. I said I would work for him for free. I desperately pleaded with him not to kill my family. He finally gave in. He accepted my offer. But before they left, one of the men used a machine gun to hit my father with it on the back. He kept hitting him hard for a long time. He ended up causing permanent damage to some of my father's spinal cord. And like Gino, the doctors could only offer him a wheelchair. They had no medical solution.' At this moment, Gino felt a little offended by the comparison between his grandfather and him. He felt that his grandfather was a victim of crime, and that he was a victim of his father's misconduct. He hated his father for his selfish decision to drink and drive. Gino had always hoped that his father would one day become a cripple, so that he could exactly relate to his pain.

Gino silently wheeled himself backwards, and left the room to cyber chat with his friends from Youth camp. He was no longer interested in his father's whole story. He had never fully trusted or believed in his father. Gino knew that his father had always exaggerated his stories in the past. Both Sylvana and Tony had not noticed Gino's exit, they were spellbound by Dominic's story, especially Sylvana, seeing that she was his wife for so many years, and he had never told her much about his past.

'Well, from then on I worked for Antonio. I did the odd job here and there. I helped to smuggle weapons and drugs from place to place. As a kid I got away with all the parcel deliveries. Sometimes, I did not know what was in the parcel, but I knew I had to keep working for Antonio to protect my family from him. This went on for many years, and then my father died. And I was too involved with some of the group's dealings, I could not go back. Besides, I had to take care of my mother and two young sisters.' Dominic said, and used both hands to wipe his tears.

'So Papa, Are you saying that the business, the house is all built from dirty money?' Tony was quick to ask, and not too pleased with the idea that his father was a gangster.

'No, Tony. No. No, my son. Everything we have here in America comes from clean money.'

'How? I don't understand, Papa', Tony anxiously kept probing into the family's past. He wanted some detailed answers from his father, in order to satisfy his curiosity.

'You see I was never proud, and never happy working for Antonio. Antonio was a very, very bad man. And you know what they say son. My father once told me, a man who does not fear God, then one must fear him. Half the Sicilian Polizia were corrupted by Antonio. I decided to flee from my past by joining a cruise liner filled with refugees waiting to sail off Sicily's sea shores. This was the only way I was going to be free from the mafia, was for me to leave the country. When I came to L.A., I worked as a waiter at Studio Bar 66. During my work there, I met an old Jewish lady. She was a very strong lady, and knew how to live life. We had become good friends, you know, having chats sometimes at my apartment, and sometimes at her penthouse. Then one day, to my surprise, her lawyer knocked on my apartment door, and handed me important legal documents which clearly stated that I was the sole proprietor of all her three L.A. properties. I sold them and used the money to build the pasta company, restaurant and the estate.'

'Okay! I see Papa.' Tony was relieved to know that their family had not been living on crime money. Tony was very honest, and hardly missed Sunday Mass with Consuela and Fabio at St. Paul's Cathedral downtown. Sylvana felt stunned by all the information Dominic had dished out to them for the first time. She found it difficult to absorb some of Dominic's past, particularly his past times in America. This is the first time she had heard about the Jewish lady or Antonio and the mafia. He had always told her that their wealth had been accumulated from his parents' inheritance. And she had wondered if there was more to his past stories, then what he had cared to share with them. Sylvana thought that she would question him later about the past, but momentarily was very keen on learning more about the strange parcel he had received and its relevance to the past.

'So sweetheart. Tell us what those things in the box have to do with your past. And why did they upset you so much?' she looked straight into his eyes. He also had Tony's full attention.

'The black scorpion represents a member of the mafia group, of course. The sword means honour.' Dominic said, as he rolled up his shirt sleeve to reveal the tattoo on his upper arm that resembled the silver sword, which parted through the letter D and A. Sylvana knew he had a tattoo on his arm, but had never examined it very closely. Besides, Dominic had told her that the tattoo had been a special friendship inscription since his army days back in Italy.

'What does D and A stand for?' Sylvana curiously asked, taking a closer detailed look of Dominic's tattoo.

'D stood for Dominic of course and A for Antonio. It's really kind of strange. Antonio and I weren't really close friends back then. But it felt strange. There were moments were we had helped each other, and for a moment it had looked and felt as if we were friends. I don't know how to really explain this strange bond, but perhaps it has to do with our long time involvement in the mafia. Anyway, Antonio pierced this tattoo on my arm as a birthday gift. The tattoo represented honour among the group, and I was the last one to receive it. I guess it was like those school things. Initiations.' Dominic explained.

'Papa, if the sword represents honour. Then what's it doing with a dead scorpion and a black rose.' Tony asked as he sat beside his father.

'That's just it my son. The black rose represents death of course. And you put all three together; they're supposed to represent dishonour and death.' Dominic explained as his eyes grew wider.

'But how have you dishonoured the group, Papa?'

Tony asked, beginning to feel a little worried about his father's safety.

'I don't really know how. These boxes were given to members of the group who at times had deceived the mafia, and were later found shot dead in their homes.' Sylvana felt terrified in hearing what Dominic had just said. 'Lucky for me, I was never ordered to shoot anyone. I don't know why, perhaps the group thought I was young or inexperienced.'

'But Papa, can you recall anything that you may perhaps have done to upset the mafia, or perhaps to someone in that group, just before you left Italy?' Tony desperately tried to make his father think back.

'You know come to think of it, I did desert Antonio on my last mission with the mafia. Antonio did not trust some of the guys he had sent to collect crates full of minerals. These substances were used among others in some Sicilian factories to produce drugs. So Antonio wanted to do the work himself, and he took me with him. But one member of the group must of dobbed us in. So when the Polizia had come, we ran down a mineshaft, and somewhere along there Antonio's leg got stuck under a rail. He called for help, and I came back towards him. But he's foot had been badly injured, and his trousers were also stuck under the rail. It was very difficult for me to move him. But Antonio kept screaming at me to move him, but it was impossible. And I could hear the Polizia running after us. So I wrestled with Antonio, freeing myself from his arms, and kept running. I could hear some shots. I think one of the Polizia had always been after his tail, and both his partner and he must have decided to shoot him. I don't know. I just could recall two loud gunshots. Anyway, I managed to escape over the sandy terrain, and headed towards some apple orchids. And after that, I escaped by ship to America. But, I did not

26

intentionally mean to leave Antonio. The Polizia would have probably shot the two of us. Besides, this was years ago, and Antonio was way older than me. I don't think, after all these years, he would have sent me the dishonoured box.' Dominic said, and felt puzzled by the whole situation. He couldn't understand why such a box would now be delivered after so many years.

'But it could be someone perhaps trying to avenge Antonio's death.' Tony suggested, looking at his parents with great suspicion.

'But this would be silly. As your father said, it's ridiculous to assume anything after so many years.' Sylvana tried to assure them, especially herself.

But Tony was not so much convinced that this was a simple hoax, especially when the strange box had been succinctly connected with his father's past. And not to mention that the tattoo pierced on his father's left arm was a Rembrandt of the sword in the box. Tony was not totally convinced of the box being a practical joke, especially after so many years. He did not want to dismiss his father's parcel so lightly.

'I'm going to call L.A.P.D', Tony said, as he pulled out his mobile from the inside pocket of his jacket, 'I think the Police needs to be aware of this incident all the same. We'll leave the objects with them, in case they need to further investigate this matter in the future.'

'Is this all necessary son? I'm not totally convinced that I am in a great deal of danger. Perhaps someone else from the mafia has escaped to America too. And they have heard about us through the business, and perhaps this is their way of trying to make contact with me again.' Dominic assured him.

'It's okay Papa. No one is sounding the alarm yet. But I really think the Police should be aware of the box you received tonight. I'll go and see if the box is still out there in the garden. And I'll wait outside for the Police to arrive.' Tony insisted.

'Don't you need to get back to your family, Tony. At least call Consuela. She must be worried about you.' Sylvana said. He wished his mother was right, but with Consuela's hard heart and lack of sensitivity, he knew that would not be the case. In fact, Tony assumed that Consuela would have put Fabio to sleep, watched a bit of T.V. with hot coco, and later went to bed.

'It's okay Mama. I'll call Consuela, and leave after giving a statement to the Police.' Tony replied aloud, as he headed out the door and towards the top of the staircase.

Joe had just got back from the airport as Tony had made his way downstairs.

'How's Papa doing?' Joe asked.

'Oh! He'll be okay', Tony answered him, releasing a great puff of air, and ruffled his fingers through his hair. 'It's a long story. Mama will explain everything. By the way, do you know where the box that was delivered to Papa is?'

'Check outside in the trash can. I think that's where I saw Nunzio place it.' Joe said, and dashed up the staircase.

Joe entered his parents' bedroom. He found his mother sitting on the edge of the bed looking a little tired.

'How are you keeping up Mama?' taking a hold of her hand, 'Where's Papa?'

'I'm okay Joe. Your Papa is in the spa. I got him to relax a bit.' She had asked him to check up on Gino to see how he was doing. And Joe had earlier done so before entering their room. Joe explained to his mother that Gino was asleep, and she took the next fifteen minutes or so to brief him about his father's past. And just like Tony and herself, Joe seemed somewhat shocked, and totally amazed by the fact that his father was once a rebel himself. Joe felt relieved to learn the truth about his father's past. He realized that his misdemeanors in the past, where a result of some of his father's genes. It was a major help to his understanding of why he was the *different* one in the family. His mobile had rung, and his mother left him to answer, as she made her way into the bedroom en suite.

It was Nicole on the other end of the line. Nicole was Joe's American girlfriend and lover. He had kept Nicole a secret from the family for the past two years. He was well aware of his parents' disapproval of the idea of intra-marriage. Nicole had clinked onto Joe like a magnet, even though he had treated her in a non-lady like manner at parties and other outings. She had always suggested the idea of marriage to Joe, or at least for him to consider a de facto relationship, but he had constantly refused. But nonetheless Nicole remained Joe's parasite for the past two years, constantly hanging around the restaurant, and pretended to be a long lost college friend whenever a relative of Joe had dropped by the restaurant. Nicole was madly in love with Joe, and he had felt a different kind of love towards her. Joe had enjoyed her company immensely, but she failed to be a priority when it came to family affairs.

'Why are you calling me so late?' Joe angrily spoke to her. 'Didn't I tell you that tonight was an important celebration for the family?'

'When are you going to see me? I miss you Joey', she sadly spoke.

'Didn't I tell you not to call me when I'm at my parents place?'

'But baby...'

'Shut the hell up.' Joe raised his voice and closed his mobile. And seconds later Nicole had called again.

'Listen. What do you want?' Joe asked.

'I'm just missing you. I wondered what was taking you so long. I have saved you some dinner, and I was hoping that you would spend the night with me. Besides there is something very important that I need to speak to you about.' Nicole said, and remained patient, even though Joe's tone of voice was beginning to get on her nerves. Joe sometimes spent the night over at Nicole's, pretending to work late, and to have spent the night at a friend's place in Bel Air.

'Listen! Something has come up with my father tonight, and he is not feeling too well. Now stop your whining. I'll see you tomorrow at the restaurant. Okay!' Joe continued to speak in an angry tone.

'But Joey. Baby. I need you tonight', Nicole began to sound desperate and all worked up about being neglected by Joe.

'Listen! Don't ring me anymore. I said I'm busy, okay.'

'Baby. What are you getting so worked up about? I need you.'

'Listen! I said I can't come. That's it okay. So just shut up and don't ring me again.'

'Well you better come, or else I'm coming over', Nicole screamed at him.

'Are you threatening me, babe. Listen! Don't you dare step a foot on the estate or I'm going to break both of your legs.' Joe had hung up on her, and she had called him seconds later. Joe had always treated her like shit, and she had accepted it, because of the strong love she felt for him.

'You better come in half an hour, or the whole family is going to hear about your secret affairs. And I guess the good reformed Italian boy won't be so good anymore.'

'If you come, I'll break your legs. Do you hear me?'

'You better come Joe Abrucci or I'll be the one to

inform your mother about her darling half American grandchild.' Joe's eyes suddenly grew wider, and he had felt a heated rush overwhelm his whole body.

'What did you just say?'

'Yes, Joe Abrucci. I am carrying your child. I thought you'd better know. We need to make some important decisions.'

Joe remained shocked by the news. It seemed that his whole world came tumbling down all at once. He had already been all worked up by the recent competition of two successful food franchises nearby his restaurant. He had started to lose some profits in the business. And now Nicole's pregnancy had fallen upon him like a bombshell. His parents had just stepped out from the bathroom. And they could see that Joe seemed very worried and upset about something. Joe just looked at his parents for a few seconds, very stunned, and with his mouth wide open.

'Hello! Hello! Joey. Are you still there?' Nicole kept screaming from the other end of the line. Joe had completely turned off his mobile, and stared into his father's eyes. He could recall his father always threatening his children with disinheriting them from the family's fortune, if they ever considered going through with the idea of intra-marriage. And besides Joe had never for an instant pictured himself being married to Nicole, and sharing his children with her.

'Are you allright, son? You seem very pale. Is everything okay?' Dominic asked him. And before he could answer, Sylvana had asked him who he'd been talking to on the phone, as she seemed very worried and a little shaky, after seeing Joe's pale face.

'Nothing that bad, Mama and Papa. It's just one of my close friends has been in a nasty car accident. I'm just going over to the hospital to join my other friends. Please try and get some sleep. I'll see you tomorrow morning.' Joe said, and left the room. He could see his brother Tony giving a full statement to two police officers, but he had totally ignored them and ran towards his car, and drove-off to Nicole's apartment.

CHAPTER TWO

It was approximately midnight, and Joe was outraged by Nicole's cunning tactics into seducing him for a child, as he banged heavily against her apartment door.

'Open the door, Nicole. Open it now, before I break it down.' Nicole opened the door, dressed in a white satin nightie, with a champagne goblet in her right hand.

'Shushh! Baby. You'll wake up the neighbours.' She said, and walked backwards, feeling a little frightened from Joe's temper.

'This was not part of the game, Nicole. This was not part of the game.' Joe addressed her, pointing his finger at her.

'What game, baby? I love you Joey', she spoke sympathetically.

'Like hell you don't know what I'm talking about. Your plans to seduce me, for your own benefits. This is crazy. This isn't going to work. I will not let you manipulate me into marrying you. It's not on. There is just no way.' Joe frantically spoke, and stroked his hair, letting out a deep breath. Nicole had reluctantly, yet slowly crept up to him. She placed her hand on his shoulder, and he quickly shrugged it off. 'No, Nicole. Your pampering isn't going to work anymore.'

'But baby, I love you, I'm going to have your baby. Our baby.' Her eyes were consumed with tears. This had only made Joe more aggressive, as he violently smashed the lamp beside him, and grabbed her from both arms.

'You listen, and you listen good baby. You're not going to ruin my life, or my relationship with the family. You better make an appointment to have what's inside of you aborted. I will not be part of your life or the baby's. And don't come to see me at the restaurant

33

until you have had the abortion.' The look on Joe's face had really frightened Nicole. She had never seen this side of him before. He seemed like a very vicious vixen that was entrapped, and ready to be captured. Joe seemed like a totally different person to Nicole. She had always known he was dead set against marriage. She realized that her plans to play with fire had caused her a massive back draft. Joe violently shook her, and left. She fell down onto her knees, sobbing heavily, and called out to him. 'Joey. Joey. Come back. I love you. I love you Joey', she screamed.

That same night Joey had walked into the estate in a very bad mood. He caught a glimpse of Sylvana in the kitchen, and it had seemed to him that she was taking up a glass of water to Dominic.

'Is Papa allright Mama?' he spoke, breathing heavily.

'He's okay. He's just had some bad dreams about his past.' Sylvana replied, holding the glass of water in her hand. She could see that Joe was not himself, and that there seemed to be something troubling him. She realized that if he had really gone to visit a friend in hospital, he would have taken more than an hour to get back. But she thought it was best not to ask him about it. Joe seemed like a ticking time bomb that was waiting to explode.

'Do you want me to make you a sandwich?' She gently asked, as she came forward and approached him at the bottom of the staircase.

'No thanks, Mama. I'm just tired. I think I'll just go to bed.' Joe said, and dashed up the staircase. Sylvana turned off the light switch, and followed him up the stairs.

A week had passed by, Dominic, Sylvana and their two sons were being served breakfast by two maids. They were expecting Dina and Nunzio to come back from their honeymoon later that afternoon. Tony pulled up in his corvette to pick up his father for work. He didn't usually pick up his father, but they both had an important business meeting that morning before going to the company. The maid had brought in some flowers with a red-ribbon box addressed to Dominic. This had sparked a little fear in Dominic, and caused the rest of the family to feel a little unsettled. The Police were still clueless as to the significance of last week's parcel, and Tony had not revealed to them all the details about his father's past. Tony had seen the maid take the box from outside, and quickly made his way to the dining area. Dominic stared at his family in a few moments of suspense, before opening the box. He had found a happy note from his personal secretary with freshly baked brownies. They all smiled with a great sigh of relief, and Dominic continued to read the note aloud, which his secretary had basically heard that he was feeling a bit down, and she felt some of his favourite sweets would cheer him up. Sylvana had suggested that he takes her one of their preserved wine bottles as a token of the family's appreciation. And both Dominic and Tony left.

Sylvana turned to Joe and felt curious about him not being dressed for work yet.

'Are you going to work in your pyjamas?' she amusingly commented.

'No, Mama. I don't have work until mid afternoon. The head chef, Bruno, is looking after the restaurant for me.' Joe said.

'Are you feeling unwell, Joe?' Sylvana sternly asked.

'No, Mama. But every Tuesday I take the mornings off, to catch up on special errands, or see the accountant, or to catch up on some paper work. But today I'm just going to make a bubble bath and relax, before I go to work.' Joe said, and left. Joe did not want to tell his mother about some of the losses the restaurant was making. He did not want to burden his parents with the possibility of losing the business. And he was amazed that Nicole had not called him, since last week's brawl at her apartment.

'And what plans have you got today, my little Bambino?' Sylvana turned to Gino.

'I'll be on the internet talking to my friends about our athletic games at Youth camp, next week.'

'And I shall be downstairs later on enjoying a game of bridge with friends.' Sylvana said.

Early that afternoon, Sylvana was playing bridge with Sonia and some friends from the country club. The spacious, elegant lounge was filled with a lot of high class women, and the maids had decorated the lounge with antique tables filled with beverages and delicious d'oeuvres, as well as freshly brewed coffee and tea pots, and fresh scones. Upstairs, Gino was on the net with friends, and Joe had just come out of his en suite in a white bath robe. He grabbed his mobile from his bedside drawer, and dialed Nicole's number as he lay back on the bed. Joe had tried several times, early that afternoon, to call Nicole, but only got through to her answering machine. And he had even failed to reach her in his last attempt. He thought it was very unusual for Nicole not to make any form of contact with him, since the brawl. For a moment, Joe thought that perhaps Nicole had committed suicide. But then again, he realized that she was a very strong, outspoken and cunning woman. And that suicide would be the farthest thing that would come to her mind. Alternatively, Joe thought that perhaps Nicole had taken his advice about the abortion, and was perhaps doing just that. But he wasn't quite sure about the thought of abortion. He realized that pregnancy was the only strong weapon

Nicole had to keep him connected to her. He wondered what her deviant mind was up to.

Downstairs Sylvana and Sonia sat quietly giggling with the country club's president, and continued to nibble on scones. Sylvana could hear a loud racquet coming from the front door. It seemed that one of the maids was having difficulty in communicating with a female visitor. For a moment, Sylvana wondered if the woman screaming at the front door had anything to do with Dominic's past.

'I'll go and see what's going on. Please continue your games ladies', Sylvana addressed her guests with a smile. She made her way to the front door, and stood beside the maid.

'Who are you?' Sylvana asked, looking disgusted by the badly dressed woman that stood in front of her. She had also seemed to lack stable body co-ordination, and had stunk from alcohol. She had long frizzy blonde hair, blue eyes, and was bound by tight leather clothes with silver buckles, and a black high heel shoes. She seemed somewhat tartish to Sylvana.

'Who am I? I'll tell you who am I. I'm Nicole. Joey's secret girlfriend. Yes, that's who I am', she pointed to herself, as she clenched her teeth together and continued to bitterly speak, 'I'm the secret mistress of this family. But I have something now. I have a right to belong to this family. I'm sick and tired of being treated like shit. I have something now. Oh! Yes Senora, I certainly have. Where's Joey. I want to see him.' She added, forcing her way through the front door. Sylvana was completely shocked by her behaviour and attitude, and more so by the fact that Nicole was Joe's secret girlfriend. She grabbed Nicole by the arm. 'Please leave. This is not the appropriate time for your announcement. Go and spread your venom somewhere else.' Sylvana felt very angry and disgusted with her. But Nicole was certainly not willing to leave, before having seen and talked to Joe.

Nicole shrugged Sylvana's hand away, and walked closer to the staircase, screaming Joe's name.

'What are you staring at?' she screamed at one of the ladies who sat playing bridge close to her. And Nicole viciously kicked the table, and some of the women let out some screams, and stood silently shocked. Joe had witnessed Nicole kick the table as he hurriedly made his way down the staircase, fuming with great fury, and only managed to button up some of his shirt. He felt very outraged by her unexpected visit. Joe grabbed Nicole by the hair and slapped her hard onto the floor.

'Get out of my house now. Get out before I throw you out.' Joe screamed, and two of Sylvana's guests had made some shocked sounds.

'It's going to take more than this to get rid of me.' Nicole screamed at Joe, clutching onto her bleeding cut lip.

'Get out. Get out. You seductive tart.' Joe continued to raise his voice. And Sylvana had placed her arm out in front of him, trying to protect Nicole from further physical abuse by her son.

'I will no longer be kept out in the dark', she continued to scream as she slowly stood up. And Joe made his way around his mother's arm. He placed his arm under her shoulder, and pulled her towards the front door, as she continued to scream, and her high heels slid across the fine granite floor.

'No, Baby. Don't. Let go. I love you. I have something now. Everyone will understand. I love you, Joey. Please baby. Joey please. Stop it. Joey. I love you.'

'Shut up. Shut up. Go now. Go. Before I do something we'll both regret.' Joe said. He continued to make sure that his voice was louder than hers. As he distinctively knew what she had meant about having something. He knew very well that Nicole was referring to her baby. He had hoped she did not say something about her pregnancy, or it would surely have added icing to the cake. He felt Nicole's melodramatic scene in front of his mother's important guests was already bad enough, let alone for Nicole to announce their illegitimate baby in public.

'I love you, Joey. I love you, baby.' Nicole continued to raise her voice, as she sobbed, and got into her tiny Mini Cooper. Joe was very angry with her, and he probably would have killed her, if he was given half the chance.

Sylvana stood shocked and very humiliated, as Sonia escorted their guests out the front door. Gino sat in his wheelchair, also feeling very shocked, from the top of the staircase. He couldn't believe that Joe was secretly seeing an American, despite his father's forewarning of disinheriting his children. Sonia gently tapped Joe's shoulder, who stood silently beside her at the front door, and walked up to Sylvana and gave her a gentle kiss on her cheek, and told her that she would call her later, and left. Joe turned to his mother who stood at the bottom of the staircase.

'I'm so sorry, Mama.' He helplessly looked at her. But Sylvana was not in the mood to have a discussion with him. She was very disappointed in him, and slowly made her way up the staircase without a word. Joe had felt very guilty about his mother's disappointment, and drove off to the restaurant at high speed.

Later that same afternoon, Nunzio and Dina had arrived back from their honeymoon. One of the maids had told Dina about Nicole's early dramatic scene. And Dina was shocked that Joe had been secretly seeing someone in the past. Nunzio had told Dina to go up and check on her mother, while he took the travel bags up to their room. Nunzio and Dina were going to stay a few months at the estate, until their grand Old Victorian Cottage was completely built and furnished in Bel Air. The Cottage was a wedding gift to them from her parents. Her father had spoilt Dina, because she had always been daddy's only little girl over the years, or as Dominic would put it – his little darling Ballerina.

Nunzio had unexpectedly entered Gino's room, only to find him beside his dressing table snorting smack. Gino attempted to place his arms on top of the cocaine, but Nunzio very well knew that Gino was not playing with talc powder.

'What's that you've got there, champ?' Nunzio directly spoke to him, and moved closer towards the dressing table.

'Nothing, it's just some safe, simple smack that my friends shared with me at Youth camp.' Gino nervously spoke.

'You know there is nothing safe about that stuff, and it's a very uncool thing to do.' Nunzio sat at the edge of his bed with a slight grin. 'How long have you been taking this stuff?'

'Oh! Not too long. Just since two months ago. But only sometimes. I have tried it two times before, and this is now the third time.' Gino said. He felt very ashamed being caught by his newly wed brother-in-law, even though he had got to know him well before the wedding ceremony.

'You know you shouldn't be doing this. This is dangerous stuff. You don't know when a person may O.D. You can never be sure what this stuff is mixed with.' Nunzio tried to warn him.

'My friends say it's helps you to relax. That it helps you to get away from your problems. And that it makes you feel as if you are in another world, feeling very light and happy.' Gino reluctantly explained.

'But what problems do you have. I hope you're not still on about your paralysis. I thought we had discussed this many times before. You have to believe that you're a very bright, young man. And there still remains many open avenues for you to explore as you get older, regardless of the fact that you're life bound to a wheelchair.'

'But not the options I want Nunz. The accident has sure crushed my hopes of becoming a champion baseball player, let alone my desire to play in a lot of sporting events. It's all Dominic's fault. I hate him. I hate him.' Gino began to heavily sulk, placing both hands against his face. Although Nunzio knew that Gino did have a limited range of options in life, considering his handicap, however he always had made an attempt to lift Gino's spirits.

'Come on, now. There's no need for that champ. You are a handsome young man, and you have a lot of people that love you. You must always think positive. There are many quadriplegics out there who have made great achievements. You'll see how things will become better as life goes on. Who knows with your bright grades, you can go on to university to study sport medicine. That will combine your brains with your interests. Now that's a thought you may like to consider.' Nunzio reassured him, as he got up to open the bedroom door.

'Thanks Nunz', Gino quietly said, 'Are you going to tell Dina and everyone about this?' He had referred to the cocaine on the dressing table.

'Let's just say, you get rid of this stuff, and that you owe me one pal, big time.' They both grinned as Nunzio left.

Dina had met Nunzio out in the hallway, and had

41

explained to him how her mother felt petrified and humiliated by Nicole's visit. And that she was more concerned about Dominic finding out. Her mother was worried about the great damp this was going to put on Joe's relationship with his father. Sylvana could not place Joe's secret love affair under the carpet. She knew that in time some of her guests would tell their husbands, who happened to be Dominic's close business colleagues. For now, Dina had explained to Nunzio that her mother had just wanted to rest, after having taken two aspirins. And Nunzio agreed that his mother-in-law needed to rest after such shocking news.

Dina had offered to make Nunzio a light snack, before family dinner later that night. But Nunzio felt that he could no longer neglect some of the paper work that he had left back at the office prior to their wedding.

'Are you going to take long, honey?' Dina worriedly asked. She wanted the whole family to be present at dinner, since they had only come back from the honeymoon.

'I won't be long, babe. Besides I'll come back with Tony and your father.' Nunzio assured her.

CHAPTER THREE

Later that same afternoon, Nunzio had arrived at the pasta company, and witnessed a big brawl between Tony and his wife, Consuela. It was war of the roses. Tony and Consuela had been at each other's throat for weeks now. But this was the first time that Consuela had initiated a full on argument with Tony at the office. Consuela was becoming fed up with Tony constantly being consumed with the business. She was becoming very bored with her monotonous daily routines. She had become very tired of handling family affairs, and she had been planning a family vacation for weeks now, and time had never suited Tony. It was always business, business, business. And she had had enough of Tony's busy work life. She had argued with Tony that they needed to spend some quality time together as a proper family, with their son Fabio. But as usual, Tony refused to give into Consuela's idea about the need for a family vacation. He was adamant about leaving family vacations until the end of the season. And Tony had abruptly left the office, not noticing that Nunzio had stood beside his office door.

Consuela remained seated in the office, sobbing heavily, and using her handkerchief to blow her nose. Nunzio had silently entered Tony's office, and gently placed his hand onto Consuela's shoulder.

'It's okay! We all have our ups and downs. But we have to keep being strong, and mostly patient. Patience is the key factor to success. He'll end up coming around for the vacation.' Nunzio grinned at her. She had assumed Nunzio had overheard parts of their conversation, considering that they were very loud during their heated argument.

'Oh! I don't know how to get through to him anymore', she continued to sob, 'It's like he's becoming more hard and cold. Tony is constantly thinking about the business, and nothing else. He seems to always be immersed with paper work, and he even brings his business work home. It's like he's got no time for his wife and son anymore. We've become alienated from his corporate lifestyle. He no longer shows any interest in his son. I mean his son hovers around him at home, while he sits fiddling with his lap top on the dining table. I really just don't know what to do anymore. Life is getting harder and harder.'

Consuela may have sounded the neglected housewife, but the fact is she always tried to act the innocent one in her family stories. She wasn't really interested in Tony's affection, but rather her European holiday. She had always gone on day trips and shopping sprees while Tony was at work. And she knew very well that there lack of affection and communication had been going on for two years now, ever since Fabio was born. There was nothing new about their distant relationship.

'Just hang in there, Consuela. You're a strong, tough woman. You're like Dominic and I, we share strong Sicilian blood, and we always find our way around our problems.' Nunzio said, and passed her his handkerchief with a smile.

'Oh! Thanks Nunzio. I needed someone to talk to. Why can't all men share your sensitivity and wisdom.'

'Oh! Stop it. You're making some sort of a masculine hero. Look I'm blushing.' They both laughed, and Nunzio used his index finger to wipe Consuela's tear from the corner of her eye, and they momentarily stared into each other's eyes as Nunzio brushed his finger up and down her rosy cheek. Her eyes seemed to cry out for help, and her sympathetic look, somewhat had indicated to Nunzio that she had been yearning for passionate love.

'Anyhow, I better head back to my office. Listen, if you ever need to talk, I'm a good listener', he smiled, and left, also leaving Consuela with a blushing look and smile.

Later that evening, the Abrucci family gathered at the estate's grand dining table, filled with various Italian cuisines. There were freshly made Agnolotti with Spinach and Ricotta, spicy Tortellini, just the way Dominic had preferred them, and of course Dina's favourite – Lasagna. All members were comfortably seated, and Sylvana was relieved to see Dominic with a wide grin. And she quickly assumed that the news about Nicole had not yet reached him. Dina looked around the table and was so glad her prayers were answered to have all the family present at the table. She had always enjoyed having the family gathered for meals at the table. She grew up not used to having her father present for lunch, and felt also sad when Tony and Joe were absent at work. After Dominic had completed the family's meal prayer, Sylvana turned to Gino, and placed a big meal napkin under his chin. He hated being treated like a child, but opted to remain silent for Dina's sake, and the fact that it was her first family dinner as a married woman.

The family spent the next twenty minutes eating and engaged in short discussions between themselves. And of course, Dominic and Tony discussed business as usual. Consuela had also been invited that night, but after having another big brawl with Tony, she refused to accompany him to the estate. But Tony had also made an effort not to spoil Dina's homecoming dinner, even though he did not have much of an appetite. Tony had told his mother that Consuela was suffering from a migraine, and was resting at home. Sylvana and Joe deliberately avoided eye contact throughout dinner. Sylvana still felt very angry and humiliated since

Nicole's visit to the estate, and she felt it was still early to have it out with Joe.

Nunzio had noticed Joe's quiet withdrawal from the dinner table, just before dessert was served, and he had followed him upstairs. Nunzio knocked and entered Joe's room, and found Joe lying down on his bed, fiddling with the keys on his mobile.

'Hey! Joe. I noticed you quietly had left the dinner table. And it's not like you to skip dessert. Are you okay?'

'Oh! I just didn't feel like eating much.' And Nunzio had noticed his lack of appetite earlier on. 'I guess you've probably heard about Nicole.' Joe said.

'Oh! Yes. So that's what her name is. Oh! Well, things happen, and then we just have to find a way of sorting them out. Just remember you're not the only one with problems. But there are many people out there with major problems that you don't know of.'

'Oh! I have major problems, okay.' Joe reluctantly said.

'Everyone has someone that they care about besides their family.'

'You see, that's just it, Nunz. It's not that I don't care about Nicole, I do. But I'm not so sure I love her. It started out, as some chick I had picked up at the bar. Then it led to casual sex. And then it was as if she had gone out some nights deliberately looking for me in bars. And from then on she was like a parasite, hooked on to me. It all sort of blew out of proportion. I just found myself in a relationship, where with family and the business, I got too busy and took advantage of Nicole for casual flings. And for Nicole, it was sheer love. It was as if I was the right man she had long been searching for. I don't know. It's all so confusing. I must admit, at times I would go over to Nicole's apartment to find solace and comfort in her from family problems.

Especially in the year, before Mama talked Pops into giving me the family restaurant, when I was a rebel without cause. I had always got myself into money problems, mainly from gambling debts, and it was not only Mama that helped, but also Nicole. I mean Nicole sometimes took money off her rich parents to save my skin a few times.'

'I would say that's some hell of a chick. I can't see anyone doing this for another guy. She must love you an awful lot.' Nunzio said.

'But that's just it, Nunz. I haven't had time to think about our relationship, and what it may have developed into. I was always preoccupied in maintaining the reputation and success of the restaurant, to please Papa. And then there were times were you get immersed with family affairs. Especially the time when Tony and Consuela were thinking of getting a divorce and my parents had gone through hell trying to save the family's reputation. And then there's Nicole constantly clinging on to me. Always coming down to the restaurant, and insisting on getting more out of me, both physically and emotionally. She had proposed the idea of marriage a number of times, and I had always rejected it. And I guess I was a little selfish, because I was allowing Nicole to enter and be a part of my life at different stages. But I guess, as they say, I have a lot of love and soul searching to do. I guess it's important for me to know where I stand with Nicole.' Joe spoke with a great deal of thought.

'Yeah! I guess you have a lot of things to consider', Nunzio said, putting his arm around his shoulder.

'It's just that I have developed a great deal of hatred towards Nicole lately. Firstly, she seduces me into getting her pregnant, and claims that she is madly in love with me. Then she intrudes into my family home, after I have fought so hard to ensure that Nicole

47

remains my personal secret for the past two years. And so with the baby now, and all the other business competitions, I'm really beat. I'm so tired of everything.' Joe said, as he ran his fingers through his thick brown hair, and worriedly turned to Nunzio, with his big brown eyes.

'Don't worry about things. I'm sure everything will turn out right for you. What's this about other business competitions? Are you currently experiencing financial problems with the restaurant?' Nunzio curiously asked.

Joe had explained to him that in the past two months he had started to lose a lot of profit on the business, after the completion of a new resort and two other restaurants in Bel Air. He had explained to Nunzio how he was feeling frantic about losing the family restaurant, and was desparate to do anything to save it. Joe did not want his father to see him as a failure. He had already favoured Tony over the years, and had frowned upon Joe for his incompetence when it came to business. Nunzio had suggested in perhaps finding some ways for the restaurant to attract new customers. And Joe had already tried changing the menu, and cutting down on prices, but to no avail. And he was far too egotistic to turn to his folks for help. Nunzio had reluctantly suggested to Joe about a private gambling place in China town. He suggested to Joe that this could be an alternative to help him boost up on the restaurant's losses. Although, Nunzio had warned Joe not to get too deep or to mess around with the other players down China town. Joe liked the idea, as gambling had been a big part of his past. Nunzio had told Joe to keep the idea of China town between the two of them, and Joe whole heartedly agreed.

'Thanks Nunz for everything.' Joe said.

'As I said, don't let things get to you too much. Hopefully you won't stumble over greater finance. And the stuff with Nicole, well think about it, and if you're serious about her, I'm sure your folks will come around.'

'Thanks Nunz.'

'Anyway I'd better head back downstairs. I'm sure Dina would have saved me some dessert. Ciao.' Nunzio said, and exited Joe's bedroom.

Joe felt very intrigued by the idea of China town, and he did have some extra cash to consider playing with. Although he felt a little hesitant about gambling, the restaurant's losses had created the need for desperate measures. And Joe thought his problem with Nicole can be sorted out later. His priority now was to salvage the restaurant's finances.

While downstairs Gino had discussed with the family his latest camping trip to Canada over dessert. He had explained to his parents that this was an international event organized by Youth camps worldwide for paraplegics to participate in sporting competitions. Gino was also proud to share with the family his latest rowing triumph and the trophies he had received from Youth camp. His parents did not dare to oppose Gino's desire to compete in Canada, as they very well knew that there would be hell to pay. He had already blamed them for his paralysis, and they had carried this guilt for the past five years. Besides they thought they had at least owed him more than just the cost of a trip for their tragic mistake. Sylvana had suggested that the family would organize a going away party for Gino next week. And by then, Tony had thanked Dina for organizing this special family dinner and extended his congratulations to Nunzio and his sister, before leaving the estate.

That night, Dina was feeling a little restless during her sleep, and had extended her arm out towards Nunzio's side, only to discover that he wasn't there.

She sat up in bed, and removed her sleeping blindfold. She could see Nunzio sitting half naked opposite the dressing mirror. He was holding onto a small safety box, and stared at what seemed to be a bunch of newspaper clipping in the other hand. Dina had quietly and gently rested her chin on Nunzio's shoulder. And Nunzio was quick to place the papers among other things inside the box, and closed it. Dina felt curious about his rapid movement and more so about his heavy panting. She realized that she had very much frightened Nunzio, in what he seemed to be in a world of his own.

'What's wrong, hun? What were those things you were looking at?' Dina curiously asked.

'Nothing. Just forget about it.' She could see he was hiding something from her; by the way Nunzio had tightly clutched the safety box against his stomach. 'Nothing that you should be concerned about. Just some personal things of mine. You know important family heirlooms that carry great sentimental values', Nunzio continued to breathe heavily, 'Promise me that you would never come near this box or open it.' Dina stared at him oddly. 'Promise me. Promise me Dina', he shouted at her. She stood silently staring into his wide eyes for a few moments, and her eyes had begun to consume tears. He had upset her by his tone of voice. She rolled herself into bed without saying a word to him.

Nunzio quickly placed the safety box back inside the closet, and turned towards Dina. He lay down next to her, and gently stroked his hand down her back.

'I'm so sorry, baby. Please forgive me. I didn't mean to snap at you like that', and paused to give her a gentle kiss on her shoulder. 'There are just some secrets from my past that I do not wish to share with anyone right now, especially you. Please, try to understand that it's just very difficult for me to open old wounds.

Please forgive me, hun. Please.' Nunzio spoke, as he rubbed her shoulder. He was desperately trying to get Dina to forgive him, without having to share with her what's inside the box. Dina finally turned towards him.

'You scared me. I can understand you finding it difficult to tell me about the things in the box, for now. But I hope that you will end up sharing your secrets with me soon. I don't want us to keep secrets from each other, I prefer that we were always honest with each other.' Nunzio nodded his head with a smile, and kissed her before Dina rolled back over to the other side.

She lay a little upset from Nunzio's behaviour, and she was very worried about what secrets Nunzio could be hiding from her. And come to think of it, Dina realized that Nunzio had never talked much about his past life, nor his family. As far as she and her family knew, Nunzio had migrated from Italy, completed his business degree at U.C., and later worked at her father's company. He had just told Dina and her family that he grew up in a Sicilian orphanage, and he was later adopted by an Italian sterile couple at the age of twelve. Dina kept thinking about Nunzio's hesitation to share the secrets that lay in the box, as she finally drifted off to sleep.

CHAPTER FOUR

The next morning Joe stopped by China town before going to the restaurant. He had used his mobile earlier to let Bruno know that he was going to be an hour late. Joe had asked a couple of Asian men for exact directions to Sui Lee. Joe provided Nunzio's name to the man who stood behind a black screen. He let Joe through, and Joe noticed that he had to walk through what seemed to be a black narrow maze, before reaching Sui Lee and the other players. He had reached a small room with a tiny window. Sui Lee sat with the other players around a large table that contained black and red chips, and of course playing cards. The mass of cigar fumes had engulfed the whole room that would have made a person suffering from chronic asthma very ill.

Two large Asian men stood on both sides of the entrance, and Joe knew which one Sui Lee was from Nunzio's description of Sui Lee being a tiny, skinny bold guy, with black sunnies, and a black cigar that rested on his lower lip.

'So what you're playing for?' Sui Lee asked him. And Joe nervously replied, 'I'll cash in on a grand.' And Sui Lee had used his hand to invite him to take a seat. Joe kept glancing at his watch during the game, as he didn't want to be late to the restaurant. And forty five minutes later, Joe was very amused with his winnings. One of the bouncers stood beside Joe with an open brief case filled with bundles of one hundred dollar U.S. notes. Joe took a deep breath before reaching in his hand to collect forty thousand dollars. He had never won so much money before, after having placed a small bet. Joe thanked Sui Lee and left. And Sui Lee had invited Joe to come again for more bets.

As soon as Joe had entered his small office later at

the restaurant, he was quick to stash the black plastic money bag into the safety box. He started to gaze through the recent stocks list, when he had been interrupted by Bruno.

'Is chicken panajama okay for today's special menu?'

'Yeah! Sure. And offer free cappuccinos for the rest of the week. I think there are lots of coffee beans in the storeroom.' Joe told him, as he swayed his chair sideways to check the fax machine. There had been a couple of faxes sitting in the tray. One was from the pasta company, and the other from the bank. Joe was very disappointed. It seemed he was behind in his arrears on some of the extra reimbursements he has added to the restaurant in the past month. This had put a big damper on his earlier good mood. He had also been well aware of the number of previous liabilities and great costs incurred on the business. Joe slipped back into his recliner, and let out a deep breath, as his mind began to contemplate whether or not he should return to Sui Lee and risk his earlier takings.

Consuela came running down the hallway, as she playfully chased her two year old son, and to her surprise there stood Nunzio in his business suit, holding a bottle of champagne. They stared at each other for a few moments, and Nunzio smiled.

'After our last conversation at the office, I thought I would drop by and see how you were doing?' He said.

'Shouldn't you be at work?' Consuela smiled.

'That's true, except two of my clients had called earlier and cancelled, and I thought I'd pass by and see how you were doing. After all you seemed very upset the other day at the office.'

'Oh! How sweet. That's very kind of you. Please come in.' Consuela invited him in, opening the front security door. And Nunzio passed her the champagne bottle. 'You shouldn't have troubled yourself.'

'Oh! That's nothing. As you know my in-laws have plenty of alcohol back at the estate.'

'Please sit down. How is Dina?' she asked, lifting up her son.

'Howse things champ? Allright?' Nunzio tickled Fabio, 'Dina's fine. She had some job agency appointments to go to. She's trying to find some therapy work with kids and adolescents.'

'I was just about to put Fabio for a nap. Please, make yourself at home. I'll just be a minute. You'll find the cork screw with the champagne goblets besides the wall unit.' Consuela informed him, as she carried her son to his room.

Nunzio poured Consuela and him some champagne, and rested on the leather recliner, awaiting her return. Consuela returned a few minutes later and found Nunzio gazing at some family photo albums.

'I got them out earlier. I was reminiscing some past times, when Tony was not so obsessed with his father's business, and we would regularly go on trips. It was only since our son's birth that Tony changed as a person and he had become a distant workaholic.'

'That's a shame. I can see why you miss going on trips. These are great photos, and great sights. You both seemed very happy together.' Nunzio commented.

'I know. But those days are long gone. And our happiness together seemed to have disappeared into thin air', she sadly spoke, sitting beside him, and taking a sip of her drink. 'You know, I usually don't drink this early in the day, nor do I get any visitors.' Consuela further added.

'Well! Think of it as a special visit between two people who share similar heartaches and happy memories', Nunzio said, and took a sip of champagne. 'You know I grew up an orphan. And always dreamed of going on a vacation. And even when I was adopted at the age of twelve, my adopted father never took my mother and I on vacation.'

'Oh! How sad.'

'Yeap. Very sad. I guess I can relate to you and Fabio. But as they say, *C'est la vie*', Nunzio tiredly spoke, and refilled both of their glasses with champagne. 'You know. If you like, I can try and talk to Tony, and perhaps try to get him to come around. I sure know he certainly needs a vacation with all the time and effort he puts into the company.'

'Oh! Would you. That'll be great Nunz. I would greatly appreciate it if you tried.' Consuela excitedly said, as she put her hand on his and gave him a gentle kiss on the cheek. They stared momentarily into each other's eyes, as he tightly held onto her hand. Consuela could relate to the sad look on Nunzio's face. She could relate his past to hers. She also grew up in Sicily as an only child, and her father had also been absent from the family most of the time, also neglecting both her mother's and her needs and emotions.

Consuela immediately let go of Nunzio's hand, and let out a fake dry cough, as she leaned forward towards the coffee table, and took a very long sip from her champagne goblet. Nunzio also leaned forward close beside her, and refilled both their glasses with champagne. He smiled to her, and she felt a little awkward, reluctantly returning a small grin.

'Oh! Kids. They make such a mess', Consuela said. She grabbed the champagne goblet and knelt onto the floor to pick up Fabio's fire rescue play set.

'I think it's the kids sometimes that tie us down to an unhappy marriage.' Nunzio said, as he moved up to her with the champagne bottle. And refilled their goblets with the remaining champagne.

'Well! It's. It's sort of. Well. Mainly the vacation bit

of it, that seems to be effecting the marriage', Consuela awkwardly spoke, and moved forward to grab the last fire vehicle, but fell to her side.

They had both felt very tipsy from the alcohol they had consumed together. They both had found Consuela's fall very amusing. She tried to get up, but felt a little pain on her hip.

'Oouch! Oooh! I don't think I can move my hip.' She said with a bit of pain.

'Here let me help you. I once did Chinese myotherapy for ten weeks. It might help get rid of the pain.' Nunzio suggested, and was quick to begin massaging her right side.

'Oh! That feels good', Consuela said, releasing a deep blow of air. 'Oh! That's very nice. It seems like you know what you are doing', she added, as she kept twitching her eyes, enjoying her massage.

Nunzio remained silent and consistently moved the palm of his hand up and down her side. And without a word, he used his hand to caress her from the waistline up to her neck. She opened her big pale blue eyes, and innocently gazed into Nunzio's dominant black eyes. 'Oh! Maybe we should forget about the massage.' Consuela suggested, still feeling very tipsy from the champagne, and continued to twitch her eyes at him.

'Or maybe not.' Nunzio answered, and continued to stroke her chin and lips with his finger. Consuela remained weak in his arms, letting out continuous warm breaths, and felt a heavy rush of heat wave slither up her back. And Nunzio gave her a gentle kiss to the lips, and tilted his head back, and continued to stroke her chin and lips. 'Oh! I don't know if I should be doing this. I'll probably regret it later', she tiredly spoke, feeling very weak. The champagne had slightly confused her sense of rational, as she struggled hard to resist her entrapment of seduction and desire.

'I don't think you should resist the heartache and the neglected passion that we both feel and need.' Nunzio softly whispered into her ear, and blew a hot rush of air across her ear. She felt she sure had been denied strong hot passion from Tony, and it had been such a long time since she had made love with Tony. She sure felt very confused, sexually excited, and did not know what to do. And Nunzio's charm and seduction was sure not helping her in making the right decision.

Nunzio gently scraped the short whiskers of his beard across her cheek, and gently rested his lips beside hers. Consuela continued to feel strongly driven towards seduction and passion. And for a moment there, she thought she would blame the champagne for her non resistance, as Nunzio placed his lips tightly against hers and gave her a great big passionate kiss. They remained stuck to each other for a while, before Nunzio gently placed his arm beneath her long red hair, and lifted her up, and carried her to the bedroom.

CHAPTER FIVE

Later that afternoon, Joe felt very tired after having experienced a busy morning at the restaurant. He helped usher in regular Japanese tourists..did a regular check on the chefs and menus..handled faxed food orders..Re-ordered regular stock..and interviewed potential food delivery drivers for the business. He put his feet up, and laid his head back into the recliner chair, and let out a huge sigh of exhaustion. Joe noticed Bruno passing by his office door.

'Hey! Bruno. What are you up to?' he yelled out.

'Just attending to the cold meat truck outside for some ordered deliveries, Boss.'

'Listen, I need to get some things done this afternoon. Why don't you lock up tonight with the extra set of spare keys.'

'Yeah! No worries, Boss.'

'Ciao', Joe said, as he glanced at his watch.

A female chef had popped her head into the office to inform Joe that he needed to sign delivery forms for some beverage cases at the front cashier. Joe had found a pile of messages from Nicole beside the cash register, and scrunched them up. He stared at the messages in his hand for a moment, and decided to after all stop by Nicole's apartment to relieve his sexual drive, before heading down to China town.

Nicole stood at her apartment door feeling very elated by Joe's presence. 'Hi! Darling. Please come in', she excitedly said. Joe had just stared at her for a few moments without saying a word. And Nicole's broad grin began to diminish, as she felt a little threatened by his silence. Then to her shocking surprise, Joe had swept her off her feet, giving her a great big passionate kiss as he carried her to bed. After they had spent the next twenty minutes making wild love to each other,

Joe sat up in bed with Nicole glued beside him, caressing his hairy chest.

'I have never seen you so forceful during our love making, Joey', she surprising spoke, with a small grin. Joe remained quiet, glanced at her for a second, and got out of bed to put his pants on. 'What's wrong baby. Why don't you stay a little bit longer', she begged him. And Joe remained quiet as he then put his shirt on. But moments later Joe spoke as he was about to finish buttoning-up his shirt.

'Do you think you can get me some money of your folks?'

'I don't know baby. That could be a little difficult, Hun. My father took my mother on a European holiday last week. And they're not due back 'til after six weeks', she sadly said. Nicole felt miserable about not being able to help him. She had always given him money in the past without any questions. Her balance account was low, as she had always relied on her rich daddy to provide her with extra cash every month. 'I'm so sorry I can't help you this time. I can try calling daddy in Europe', she offered.

'Just forget it.' Joe said, and grabbed his jacket, and left. Nicole lay back in bed staring at the ceiling, as she heard Joe slam the front door.

She felt relieved that Joey had come back to her, even if it was for just casual sex. She didn't care. Nicole was happy to be part of Joe's life. She had hoped that with time, and with the baby being born, Joe would spend even more time with her. She was surprised Joe had not mentioned anything about the idea of abortion, as he was sure adamant about it last week. Nicole had hoped that this was a sign of Joe's silent acceptance of the baby. She had always dreamed of being married to Joe, and being part of the Abrucci family. She turned to the other side, and snuggled Joe's pillow against her breast with a wide grin. Even if marrying Joe was wishful thinking, she wished to maintain this fantasy, and hoped that one day her marriage to Joe would become a reality.

Later that same afternoon, Joe had parked his car outside Sui Lee's gambling maze at the back of China town. He had brought along with him ten grand, to place on higher bets, and hopefully to win big money. He had once again used Nunzio's name to get in.

'They all come back. I told you little player.' Sui Lee referred to Joe, laughing, finding it very amusing that Joe had returned to even bet on higher stakes. Joe spent his cash over the next ninety minutes right until the last dime. And by the end of the games, Joe had not only lost ten grand, but he was also way over his head in debts. Sui Lee stared angrily at Joe, as Joe sat nervous in his chair, unable to further retrieve money from his plastic bag.

'What's the matter champ? Are you going to cut your losses?' Sui Lee spoke with a grin, 'But let me remind you that you better pull out more than a rabbit out of that bag, champ. You're way in deep now, my friend. How are you going to repay Sui Lee.'

'Just give me a few weeks. And I promise to repay my losses..even with interest', Joe nervously said, 'My girlfriend's father will come back soon from Europe, and whatever profits the restaurant rakes in, I'll put them together and give them to you.'

'No. You see, this won't do champ', Sui Lee angrily slammed his hand on the table, and slowly made his way around the table to Joe. 'You see champ, Sui Lee does not work like that. You play, You pay. And you pay fast', Sui Lee let out a puff of cigar fume across Joe's face. 'But I'll tell you what kid, I'm going to cut you some slack, seeing that you are related to Nunz', Sui Lee offered Joe an alternative. 'I need a man to deliver a truck for me down by Santa Monica's Bay.'

'What sort of a delivery?' Joe was quick to ask.

'That doesn't concern you champ. What concerns you is paying back Sui Lee. And that's very important. You will meet two of my men back here, next Wednesday at five p.m.' Sui Lee said, and Joe stood up to leave. 'And don't be late.' Sui Lee told him with a serious look. Early that evening, Joe drove off to the estate, feeling very depressed and frustrated, and what seemed to be a big grey cloud hanging over his head.

CHAPTER SIX

Early afternoon, the following Wednesday, Sylvana and Dina were excitedly running around the estate to ensure that everything was in order for Gino's going away party. Sylvana was on the phone with Dominic and Tony reminding them to be at the estate by six p.m. Dina escorted the catering company into the kitchen, and they began to prepare mini hot dogs, mixed savouries, and other trays filled with pastries and sweets. The estate was swamped with different sorts of helium balloons. And Gino was in his room chatting with friends, and packing some of his belongings for camp vacation. Nunzio had just arrived from work, greeting Sylvana and Dina at the front door, followed by Joe who without a word rushed up the staircase. Sylvana thought this was a good time to have a quick word with Joe about Nicole. She felt much calmer since Nicole's visit to the estate, and she felt very confident in confronting Joe about it.

Sylvana was still amazed about Dominic being kept in the dark about it. She thought that perhaps her female guests had yet to tell their partners about the incident, or perhaps they had, and Dominic's colleagues had been too busy to recall Nicole's emotional outburst. Either way she felt relieved about Nicole being an alien phenomenon to Dominic. She excused herself from Dina and Nunzio, and followed Joe to his room. Sylvana stood beside his open door, and was shocked to find Joe packing a small travel bag.

'And where are you off to, young man?'

'Nowhere Mama, I just have to spend the next couple of days with friends in Santa Monica.' Joe said, as he continued to throw a couple of shirts in his bag.

'But what about the restaurant?' Sylvana was quick to ask, 'Who would look after that?'

'Don't worry Mama, Bruno has got everything covered.'

'But what about Gino's going away party?' Sylvana helplessly asked. She was hoping that Joe would have at least spent an hour or two with his brother, before going off with friends to Santa Monica. After all Gino was going to spend the next three months in Canada.

'I can't Mama. I have to leave in one hour. Besides I have to sort some things with Bruno back at the restaurant before I leave.'

'But why all of a sudden? Is something wrong, Joe? This has nothing to do with that girl named Nicole?'

'No Mama. It has nothing to do with Nicole. And this is not the right time to be discussing it. I am in a hurry. I've got to go now. Trust me Mama. Don't worry. We'll talk when I get back.' Joe said, grabbing a hold of his bag, and quickly brushing his mother's cheek with a kiss as he left. Sylvana could not help but worry about her son. She had this motherly instinct that her son was in some sort of trouble. And she thought that perhaps it had something to do with his girlfriend Nicole. She silently prayed that her son would be allright as she slowly headed off towards the top of the staircase.

Downstairs Nunzio and Dina had noticed Sylvana looking a little down.

'What's wrong Mama? Are you okay?' Dina worriedly asked.

'I'm okay. I'm just worried about Joe. He doesn't seem to be himself lately. And I just worry about him.' Sylvana tiredly spoke. Dina suggested that her mother assists her in checking on the caterers in the kitchen, and Nunzio had excused himself to go and change into something less formal.

Moments later, one of the estate's maids had informed Sylvana and Dina in the kitchen that their best

63

friends had awaited them at the front entrance. Sylvana happily greeted Sonia, and Dina exchanged kisses with her college friend Margaret Wheiler. Dina and her American friend Margaret had been best of friends for many years, and Margaret was well-known and well-liked by all members of the Abrucci family. Back in their schooling days, Margaret played skipping, soft ball and bike races with Dina, Tony and Joe. Sylvana turned to greet Margaret, as Dina exchanged kisses with Sonia.

'I'm a little upset with you. We hardly see you these days. You're only up the road.' Sylvana both sarcastically and amusingly said to Margaret. She was like a second daughter to Sylvana, as she had spent a lot of time at the estate during her adolescent years. And both Dominic and Sylvana had approved of Margaret, because she was witty, polite, and a family sort of a person. And that's what the Abrucci's mainly liked – family cohesiveness. Although the Abrucci's have experienced a few family crises in the past, they still wished to recognize themselves as a strong unified family.

'Oh! I've been so busy senora. I've been busy doing things, cooking for myself, working at the nursing home, and not to mention renovating the house since my parents went to visit Aunt Edna in England.' Margaret said, giving Sylvana an extra hug and kiss. Margaret had graduated around the same time as Dina as a nurse from California University. She was the same age as Dina, but was yet to settle down with her prince charming. Although she had lately mentioned to Dina that she was dating a male nurse, and that it had looked very promising.

'Oh! You are always welcome to come and eat here, my little darling.' Sylvana grinned, as she used both hands to ruffle her long brown hair from the back of her coat. Both Dina and Sonia laughed about Sylvana pampering Margaret's hair.

'You once had hair like that Sylvana, but without the grey.' Sonia amusingly remarked.

Some of Gino's friends from camp had started to arrive, and the maid had showed them to his room. Dina excused herself, as she told her mother that she'll go up and check on her husband.

'How is Nunzio by the way. I haven't seen him since the wedding.' Margaret asked.

'Oh! He's fine.' Dina left her mum with Margaret and Sonia and went upstairs to check up on Nunzio.

Dina had once again witnessed Nunzio holding his safety box as she entered their bedroom. He was standing with his back to her, once again, immersed in all the stuff in the box. It seemed as if he was in another world. And this time Dina did not dare to creep up on him, in order to avoid another fiasco. She let out a fake dry cough to attract Nunzio's attention. And he turned around, while instantly shutting the box closed. He seemed once again surprised to see her, and to be caught off guard, staring at the box.

'Have you finished putting something comfy on? When you're ready, come downstairs. Margaret and Sonia would like to see you.' Dina said, and left the room. She didn't bother to discuss the box thing with him. She did not want to spoil Gino's evening with an argument. And besides, Dina had realized that it was still early before Nunzio was willing to open up to her about his secret past. Nunzio also realized that Dina must have not bothered to say anything about the safety box, because it had been a special night for Gino and the family. He placed the box back into the wardrobe and followed Dina downstairs.

Back at the company, Tony was busy sorting out some finance papers with Dominic. He suggested that his father leaves early to get to the estate, and that he would follow him after wrapping up some extra paper work.

'Are you sure son?' Dominic said.

'Yes, Papa. I've got everything wrapped up here at the office. Get going. Besides Nunzio would probably be feeling very awkward without an older man there.' Tony assured him. Moments later Dominic had greeted some of his business colleagues downstairs, as he made his way to the car. He noticed that his car phone was ringing, and he made sure he quickly reached the car, threw his briefcase into the front passenger seat, and picked up the receiver beside him. It had turned out to be Sylvana reminding him not to be too late for Gino's party. And with a grin, Dominic reversed the car, taking a quick glance at his front driving mirror, and to his great astonishment, there was a white box with a black ribbon in the back seat.

He had instantly put on his brakes, and looked to see if there was someone watching, as he felt his heart beat faster. After realizing that there was no one in sight, Dominic used the car phone to notify Tony up in the office. Tony came rushing down the building, and to his father's car.

'Are you okay, Papa? Did you check what's in the box?' Tony asked him, trying to catch his breath back.

'No. Not yet son. I thought I'd wait until you came down. Shall we call the police, before opening it?' Dominic worriedly asked.

'No, Papa. It's okay. I'll first open it up.'

Tony had carefully opened the box, as if he was attempting to detonate a bomb. Both Tony and Dominic were shocked to see that the box had once again contained a dead black scorpion, a silver sword, and a black rose – except this time, the box had also contained a dead rat with its throat slit.

'This is the joke of one sick bastard. And if I ever get my hands on that son of a bitch, I'll punch the living daylight out of him.' Tony angrily said, smashing his fist against his father's car.

'Take it easy, son. Let's not ruin Gino's going away party. I'm sure it's just someone's idea of a sick joke. As I said last time to you and your Mama, it's probably someone from my past, trying to make contact with me, through what they see as a practical joke.' Dominic tried to reassure him. But Tony remained staring at the ground, looking very worried about the second package, especially with the addition of a dead rat.

'C'mon son. I'll be fine. You go and finish the paperwork, and I'll see you back at the estate.' Dominic said, patting Tony's shoulder.

'Okay, Papa. But be careful on your way home.' Tony said, as he watched his father drive out onto the main road.

CHAPTER SEVEN

Back at the estate, Consuela had arrived with Fabio, and was greeted by both Dina and Nunzio outside on the front patio. Consuela had kissed Dina with a smile, and hardly shook Nunzio's hand, avoiding any form of eye contact with him. This was the first time she had seen him, since they were both drunk, and she had later woken up naked in bed to the cries of Fabio. Dina did not give second thoughts to the strange look that had suddenly appeared in Consuela's eyes, and followed Consuela into the estate holding a wine glass. Nunzio's face had gone a little pale, and he had hoped that Consuela had not mentioned anything to anyone. Besides, he realized that if she did, they would both stand to lose everything. He remained on the front patio, and lit up a cigarette. Nunzio was desperately trying to quit smoking, but it was moments like this which he felt he can do with a drag or two.

Dominic had pulled into the estate's car port, and later inside decided not to upset Sylvana with the news about the second package. He had promised himself to make Gino's evening a happy and memorable one. More of Gino's adolescent friends had arrived onto the estate, and soon everyone started to nibble on food and to enjoy the party. Tony had also arrived at the estate only minutes ago, and was dancing with his son, beside the stereo. Dina had a big grin on her face, as she stood with Margaret outside on the back patio.

'What's that grin I see on your face?' Margaret asked, pointing at her mouth.

'Oh! I'm just happy about Gino's special night', Dina smiled.

'So how is marriage life? And how did the honeymoon go?' Margaret said, gently poking Dina's side with her left elbow.

'Well Missy, for your information, it went quite well. Hawaii's sceneries were spectacular, and watching the Honolulu dancers beside the fire on the beach with Nunzio felt pretty amazing.'

'Well you know what I mean. How was it? You know losing your virginity and making love for the first time in your life. I know how some Italians are very strict in guarding their chastity. And I know you, you never gave any second thoughts to boys in college.' Margaret amusingly said.

'Oh! Don't be so disgusting', Dina laughed, taking a sip from her wine glass. And Margaret's blue eyes remained wide open, curious to know about Dina's sexual encounter with Nunzio.

'Well! It's difficult to say how I felt. I mean it was kind of quick, and it seemed as if Nunzio had gone through sexual intercourse, without really being there. I don't feel there is much passion being ignited during our love making. It's like another simple thing that Nunzio feels he has to do. Besides we had only had a second encounter since returning from Hawaii. Nunzio never initiates our love making, nor does he seem to be into foreplay. He forcefully enters me with a cold expression on his face. Sometimes I get a little scared from his absent view during our love making'. Dina hesitantly spoke, but she felt comfortable in confiding in her best friend. Margaret was more than just a friend; she had been like a sister to Dina over the years.

'So it seems like Romeo has the looks, but fails to play the game right. Well hopefully he'll come around, or poor you. Poor Dina. Not much fun in the romance department can be a great bore in a girl's life.' Margaret smiled, and pinched Dina's cheek. And they both put their arms around each other as they re-entered the party scene back inside.

Later that night, Nunzio decided to join Consuela in

the kitchen to grab extra ice, leaving Dina to dance with her brother Tony. Consuela had noticed Nunzio follow her in, and she made a great effort to browse through the freezer without looking at him. But she felt very awkward ignoring him, when Nunzio remained standing still behind her, taking sips from his wine glass.

'I guess it can get very warm on party nights', he bent forward and whispered close beside her. Consuela did not say a word, feeling a little awkward from Nunzio's presence. She quickly placed some ice cubes into a glass bowl and walked away. Nunzio quickly followed her and grabbed her by the arm.

'Listen. I don't have any regrets about the other day. What happened had just happened, and it was obvious that we both had a good time. Let's just keep this our little secret, or else we both have got a lot to lose.' Nunzio whispered closely into her ear, and tightly squeezed her elbow.

'It was just a bloody big mistake. We were both tipsy, and did not know what we were getting ourselves into.' Consuela nervously spoke, shrugging her elbow away from him, and wiped a tear drop as Dina walked into the kitchen. Consuela just marched out of the kitchen without a word, leaving Nunzio to explain a lie to Dina who had a blank face, as she stared at the two of them.

'What's all that about?' Dina asked, looking like she required an answer. And a good one for that matter.

'Oh! It's nothing we should involve ourselves in', Nunzio said, as he put his arm around Dina, 'The other day at the office, I overheard Consuela and your brother having an argument. She blames Tony for being constantly preoccupied with work, and that he never shows interest in his family life. So Consuela is very upset because apparently she had been planning this

70

vacation for a while, and it is yet to happen. So I chatted with her about it last time at the office, and now we just talked about it a little.'

'Oh! Poor Tony. I didn't know my brother was experiencing some marital problems. He always puts on a strong exterior. But then again he is a bit like Papa. They find it difficult to share their emotions with others.' Dina sadly spoke.

'Now, you don't worry your pretty little face about it. These are little things that concern Tony and Consuela only. And besides, it's best they work out these sorts of things between themselves. Don't worry babe, things will work out for them. I'll have a chat to Tony, and try to get him to take a vacation.' Nunzio said with a smile.

'I'm so glad that you try to help people, sweetheart. That's one of the things I admire in you.' Dina said, giving him a gentle kiss to the lips, and left. Nunzio had taken a big sip from his wine glass, relieved that Dina had accepted his story, and followed her to the lounge.

An hour later, after the family had shared some of the party cake with guests, most of Gino's friends had left. Consuela informed Tony that she was experiencing migraines, and left early with Fabio, to avoid being in the same room as Nunzio any longer than she had to. And that worked well for Consuela seeing that she had come to the party in her own car. A few minutes later, the rest of Gino's guests had left, leaving him to spend some time with the family. By then Sylvana and Tony were having a slow dance together, Dina and Nunzio stood beside Gino's wheelchair chatting with him, and Dominic was resting on the lounge room setter with a glass of white wine, immersed in his deep thoughts about the second package he had received earlier, back at the company.

'A call for you senora. It's your brother, Joe', the

housemaid informed Dina.

'Hello! Joey. Hello!' Dina was experiencing some difficulty in the phone reception, 'Joe can you hear me?'

'Listen, I need your help', Joe's voice sounded as if he was speaking from a far distance.

'What's wrong? Where are you?' Dina's worried look had led the whole family to sense that there was something wrong.

'I need you and Tony to come down to Santa Monica Police station', she could sense trouble in his voice, 'I'm in big trouble ‚Sis. I've been charged with possession of drugs.'

'Oh! My God, drugs?' Dina's voice grew loud, 'But why? How?'

Sylvana clinged tightly onto Tony's arms with great distress. And the whole family had their eyes fixed on Dina with great anticipation.

'I haven't got time to explain. Please hurry. Come down with Tony.' Joe said, and hung up. The family had made their way closer to Dina.

'This was Joe. He's been charged with drugs in Santa Monica', Dina said, staring shockingly towards the floor.

'What? What's Joe doing in Santa Monica? And what's this about drugs?' Dominic said. He could not believe what he had just heard.

Dina grabbed her coat and passed Tony his jacket. 'He wants us to drive down there', Dina told Tony. Dominic offered to come along, but Tony thought it was better if he stayed with Sylvana, until they had learnt more about Joe's current situation. Besides, he thought the long drive would make his father very tired. Dina told Nunzio to stay with her parents, in case he needed to do something for them back home, and she yelled out to him to keep his mobile on as they left.

During their drive down to Santa Monica, Tony made two calls via his mobile. The first call was to inform the family's attorney to meet them at Santa Monica Police, and he later called Consuela to inform her about what's happened with Joe, and that he was going to be very late. That night Nunzio and Gino went upstairs to their beds, and Dominic followed them a little later. Sylvana wished to remain on the lounge recliner, awaiting a call from either Dina or Tony. Sylvana prayed and hoped that everything would go well for Joe, and that there would be no need for the American Italian community to learn about this family predicament.

CHAPTER EIGHT

Down at Santa Monica Police headquarters, Joe was escorted by a police officer into the interview room. He felt very ashamed of himself, as he sadly looked at Dina, Tony and the family's attorney awaiting him at the table. Dina stood up and ran up to Joe, and gave him a big hug. Tony remained seated, looking very disappointed in Joe, and felt humiliated in front of the family's attorney by what his brother had done. He felt like punching the living daylights out of Joe, but at the same time, realized that it wasn't the appropriate course of action at this moment in time. The attorney had explained the police reports and legal charges pending on Joey. Dina and Tony had learnt that their brother had gambled, and was unaware that the delivery truck was loaded with cases of various amphetamines and other illegal substances.

Their attorney had explained the severity of the charges, and later told Tony that the police have charged Joe on two accounts – for possession of drugs, and attempting to transfer a substantial amount of various narcotic substances.

'So what happens next?' Tony worriedly asked the attorney.

'Well I'm going to see about getting the prosecution to shift the case back to Beverly Hills, and I will have to apply for bail, before his upcoming trial, which won't be until three months down the track. Now we need to ransom family property as bail surety, as bail in this case would be somewhere over one hundred thousand dollars', the attorney sternly suggested to Tony outside the interview room, while Dina remained at the table comforting Joey.

'Well! I guess there's Joey's restaurant we can put up for bail', Tony said.

'Well! Your brother has said in his statement that there seems to be a bank title withholding the restaurants financial liabilities and assets. So I'm afraid that won't do. Perhaps you need to discuss with your parents about putting up the estate for Joe's bail.' Tony nodded, and the attorney continued to talk. 'Now I'm afraid Joey will have to remain in custody until the bail hearing in two weeks, but he will be allowed visits and some clean clothes deposited into his name. And also you would need to leave him perhaps a hundred dollar note before you leave, so that he is able to call the family back at the estate.'

Later Tony had called Sylvana, who had anxiously awaited their call back at the estate. He had briefed her on Joe's legal situation. And Sylvana wept, and without hesitation agreed to put up the estate as bail surety. Tony had informed Sylvana that there was nothing much that Dina and himself could do for Joey at this stage, and that they would soon be heading back to Beverly Hills. Sylvana had felt a little startled by Nunzio's presence at the bottom of the staircase, as she placed down the phone's receiver.

'Sorry to startle you senorita. So what's the word on Joey? What did Dina and Tony have to say?' Nunzio quietly spoke, and moved up closer to her.

'Well all I could really work out from Tony's call, is that Joe is in big trouble with the Santa Monica Police. Something about Joe being caught driving a truck full of drugs. And that our attorney is busy trying to get Joe bail.' Sylvana nervously said before crying uncontrollably.

'Don't worry senora. Everything will work out for Joe. I'm sure his attorney will help him out. Please calm down until Dina and Tony return with more details. I'm sure Joe has been a victim of crime. Besides you need to be strong for the family. In times like these we have to be tough.' Nunzio tried to comfort her.

'I don't understand, Nunzio. My Joey, you know, he's done some bad things in the past, here and there, but not as bad as this. I don't believe he would do such a thing. Not drugs anyway. I just want my son to come back home and safe. I just want my son to come back to me.' Sylvana helplessly looked at him, and her eyes overwhelmed with tears, while Nunzio remained staring at the ground. He had hoped that Joe had not said anything to Tony or Dina about him suggesting China town as a way to relieve his financial debts. He knew the family would be very upset with him, especially Dina. He felt Dina would never forgive him, if Joe was to go to prison. And Nunzio feared being castrated by the Abrucci family.

The next morning Tony and Dina had arrived at the estate. Inside Dominic and Sylvana sat quietly at the breakfast table. They were too worried about Joe, and could not find the appetite for scrambled eggs and sausages. Although, Gino sat stuffing his mouth with sausages at the other end of the table. He was oblivious to the severity of Joe's case back in Santa Monica. Sylvana had only told Dominic about Joe's case when she had returned to her bed last night, and they had both decided to keep Gino in the dark, so as to not spoil his camping trip. He had been looking forward to it, and was excitedly digesting his breakfast, awaiting the camp bus to arrive at the estate. Besides, Sylvana and Dominic knew that Gino would be heartbroken about Joe, as Gino had only felt comfortable in confiding with Joe about his handicap over the years.

Tony had walked in to inform Gino that the camp bus had arrived, while Dina remained outside grabbing her coat from the back seat. Sylvana escorted Gino to the front door, assisting him in collecting his travel bags at the front door. He hurriedly wheeled himself towards the bus, as one of the maids promptly followed him with his cap and coat. Gino quickly waved goodbye to Dina and Sylvana, as he made his way up the bus ramp. Dina turned to her mum, and gave her an enormous hug, as they both wept uncontrollably for a few moments. They later went inside and joined in on Dominic and Tony's discussion about Joe. Tony had explained Joe's legal situation to the family in detail.

After having heard what Tony had to say about Joey's case, Dina suggested that she'll go up and check on Nunzio. And Sylvana headed off towards the kitchen, to inform the maid to make five cups of freshly brewed Italian espresso coffee.

'Papa. There is also something else that I think you should know about', Tony said, as he ruffled one of the meal serviettes in his hand, 'The attorney had also told me that Joe has accumulated a lot of debt on the family restaurant.'

'Oh! Joe was never the business type. Your mother had talked me into letting Joe focus on the restaurant business. So I'm not surprised. I knew something like this would happen sooner or later. Your brother never thinks. I mean look at what he's got himself into now', Dominic said, letting out a deep breath, 'I guess I'll go over now to the restaurant, and I will discuss this matter with Bruno. I'll also have to raise Bruno's pay, so that he can look after the restaurant, while I juggle some other work from the business.'

'Papa. Have you said anything to Mama about the second parcel?' Tony asked.

'No son. Let's just keep quiet on this trivial thing. There is already enough going on with the family, now that Joe's trial is coming up. Besides I don't want your mother to worry more than what she has too. Now, you go son, and see to your family. Get some sleep, and complete all business negotiations tomorrow.' Dominic tapped him on the shoulder. Sylvana had returned with the coffee tray, as Tony was making his way to the front door.

'Aren't you going to stay for coffee, Tony?' she asked.

'No, Mama. I'm very tired. I need to get some sleep.'

'Besides, Tony needs to get back to his family, sweetheart.' Dominic yelled out from the dining room.

'Okay! Son. Drive carefully, and give Fabio a kiss from me.' Sylvana told Tony.

Later that afternoon, Tony woke up to Fabio hitting him with a soft toy. He gave his son a big bear hug, and a kiss, as he got out of bed. He carried Fabio with him over to the kitchen, where Consuela stood cooking beside the stove. Consuela had told Tony that she was sorry to hear about Joey. She had spoken to Dina earlier over the phone. And Tony had filled her in on Joey's legal situation. And just like the rest of the family, Consuela was puzzled as to why Joe was driving a truck full of drugs in the first place. Tony assumed that his brother had made a deal to deliver the truck for an exorbitant price, so that Joe could pay off some of his debts. But, Tony explained to Consuela that it was still early to judge Joe's position, until he revisits him back in Santa Monica.

Consuela had cooked Tony's favourite, Ravioli Carbonara, to help ease her way into discussing their next family trip. It was quite a while since they had a family dinner together. They had usually argued most days, and Tony went over to his parents for dinner. He had always made it out to the family that Consuela had given him her full blessings to have dinner at his mother's. And although Sylvana and Dominic felt suspicious about Consuela's absence at times, they did not wish to meddle in their son's marital life. After all they knew what sort of a person Consuela was. To Tony's parents Consuela was the wicked witch from the west, and Fabio was her hostage.

Consuela romantically glanced across the table at Tony who sat busily twirling pasta into his fork. Consuela had let out a dry fake cough before she spoke.

'You know, I think it's great how you are looking after the family at a time like this.' Her statement had come as quite a shock and surprise to Tony. In the past he had only recalled Consuela, screaming at the top of her lungs, how selfish he had been, always neglecting his second family for the first. She had always vindictively screamed about him being immersed in business work and family affairs, and how he did not give her or Fabio the time of day. But at the same time, Tony had not recalled having dinner with his wife in such a long time. He felt it was a weird late afternoon, sitting opposite his wife over an early dinner, Consuela constantly flashing smiles at him, without them tearing each other's hair out. And with all the peace, and no arguments between them, Tony for a moment had thought that perhaps he was asleep, and had not woken up yet.

Fabio had come up to him, making motorized sounds with his big red jeep. Tony had put Fabio onto his lap, and began to share his food with him.

'You know, it sounds promising that Joe will be out on bail soon. And you would be relieved to see him back at the estate. And you know you have wrapped up many of the end of season business work. So perhaps it would do you good to spend sometime, you know darling, to clear your head from family, from work, and to spend sometime away on a vacation.' She grinned.

'Oh! I don't know, Consuela. My parents will still need me to help them sort all of Joe's legal affairs. And besides, there is already a stack of new business ventures which will require immediate attention, once the current projects are finalized.' Tony said, and continued to nibble on his food. Consuela felt very angry by Tony's usual casual attitude to dismiss the idea of a family trip, but she attempted to remain clam, and not to throw another tantrum so soon.

'But darling. There would be Nunzio and Dina, and besides Joey himself, to help your parents sort out all the legalities with the family's attorney. And you don't want to fall into a big pool of stress. Besides, Fabio, you and me won't need to go somewhere far. It could be a short trip, perhaps to some beach resort right here in L.A. Or we could spend sometime up in the mountains. Huh! How does that sound.' She quietly spoke, as she reached out to rub his hand.

'Oh! I don't know Consuela. With all that's going on back at the estate. With work. And with me needing to inspect the finishing touches to Dina's cottage soon. And there will be a special family celebration to follow. I would need to be present for the family dinner, especially for Dina. You know how Dina feels about these things, especially with Joe being inside.' Tony calmly said, and this had further provoked Consuela's anger.

'Look it's as simple as that. You grow up. You get married. You sometimes be there for your family. But there are also times when you need to make sacrifices for your marital life, and your own family. It's a simple equation. It's as simple as that Tony. Now I really can't see why you can not go on a short nearby trip with your family. Your family, Tony.' Consuela sarcastically seemed to speak, and there was somewhat an angry pitch in her tone of voice.

Tony was beginning to sense a furious confrontation between Consuela and him. He put Fabio down to play, and attempted to remain calm. And his silence was certainly aggravating Consuela's temper. She stared at Tony with wide eyes, and Tony remained silent as he used his fork to play with the remaining Carbonara. And Consuela turned her attention and anger at her two year old son.

'Look what you've made, a big mess on your new sweater. Naughty boy.' Consuela screamed at Fabio, and used a napkin to wipe off some of the Carbonara on his red sweater.

'Don't take it out on our son, Consuela. I won't let you.' Tony sternly said.

'And since when did you care about your son, or anything this family had said and done for that matter. Oh! You're quite a joke Tony Abrucci.' Consuela screamed. The wicked witch from the west was beginning to reveal her true colours.

'Just don't take it out on our son, okay.' Tony firmly remained in his seat clinging tight onto his knife and fork.

'I'll do whatever I like, since I'm the one that seems to be spending most of the time with Fabio. And since I'm the one always taking care of the family's side of things', she continued to scream, even louder this time, and Tony had lost his patience.

'Well, what a fricken time to be suggesting a bloody family trip at an inappropriate time', Tony stood up and threw his napkin onto the table, 'You know, you sure rate number one for sensitivity. You're inconsiderate. My family is going through a rough time, and you're thinking about a trip. You know, you're very understanding, oh! Yes-sir-ree. You're a very understanding woman, Consuela', his voice continued to grow louder.

'Oh! Look whose calling the kettle black. I'm not very understanding', Consuela screamed, clenching hard her teeth, and pointing to herself, 'Oh! I'm not very understanding. Well! I'm the one that spends twenty four hours with your son. I'm the one that runs around attending to family errands. I'm the one that is always taking care of the family side of things. And you're always immersed in your precious business work. You're the one who's not very understanding', she stood close beside him, staring at him with vicious eyes, as if Tony had been confronted by a venomous cobra ready to attack.

'Well! My family is going through a very rough time. My mother is very worried about Joe. My father recently received another mysterious package at work with a dead rat having its throat slit open. And my father does have a history of heart stroke, and with all what's happening he is most likely to incur another one. So I'm going to be there for my family, whether you like it or not.' Tony shouted at her, grabbed his car keys, and left. Consuela was overwhelmed with anger, that she had picked up one of Fabio's toys and threw it at the door after him.

'You can go to hell, Tony Abrucci. I hope you rot in hell. I hate you. I hate you. Damn you and your family.' Consuela screamed from the top of her lungs, as she moved a little forward towards the front house window, stricken with tears and rage.

Tony had driven down town to a nearby café, to get away from Consuela. He ordered an espresso, and was glad to see his work secretary Kerri sitting by herself at another table. He decided he would go over to her for a chat.

'Hello! Stranger. Long time no see', Tony amusingly said with a grin.

'Don't tell me, you've also been ditched by your first date', Kerri sarcastically said with a smile.

'Oh! Sorry. I didn't know you were awaiting

82

company.'

'Don't be silly, I'm only joking. Take a seat', she was so glad to see him, as he had been to find her at the café. Kerri was not only his secretary, but a personal friend since his college days. 'I was meant to catch up with Auntie Eileen over coffee, but she had called me earlier to say that she couldn't make it. She suddenly found herself having to baby sit my Cousin Michelle's daughter. Apparently Michelle had to go and see her gynecologist', she explained.

'So how's things with you these days? I hope your father has not received any more of those weird packages.' Kerri asked. Tony had always felt comfortable in confiding in her about family issues. Over the years, Kerri had been like a personal therapist to Tony during all his family crises. He would sometimes go looking for her to discuss some of the things on his mind. Tony had found it a great relief to share his family problems with her. And for many years they had both been close intimate friends. Kerri had also at times discussed her personal life with Tony, and she had always appreciated his advice. She had found him to be a very good listener, and someone who had always had the answers for others, but not for himself. Kerri saw Tony as the long lost older brother, who her family had never heard from, after her brother Jake had left home at the age of sixteen.

'Actually, my father had found another parcel in the car the other day.' Tony sadly said.

'Oh! No. Poor thing', Kerri was prompt to respond, 'And how is your father taking all this?'

'Oh! He's hanging in there. Papa is tough. And this does not come as a surprise, considering his past.'

'Yeah! I know. You told me. So could it be just a practical joke from someone trying to make contact with your dad.'

'Oh! I don't know. As you know, that's what Papa thinks', Tony said, as he took his espresso from the waitress, 'To be honest, I don't feel like it's a practical joke. I have this instinct that Papa is likely to experience danger somewhere later down the road.' He took a sip of his hot espresso.

'So why aren't you dressed so formal, today? It's not like you to be in jeans and t-shirts.' Kerri tried to cheer Tony.

'Well you can only have one guess. Consuela and I had a brawl. She's so insensitive. She wants us to go on a trip in the middle of my family's crises.' They both smiled.

'Oh! That's a shame. But we both know Consuela's temper tantrums are always to be expected', Kerri said. She had always wanted to tell Tony to divorce her, but she was reluctant to, because of Fabio. She did not like to wreck people's homes. Kerri was still to overcome some of her deeply embedded pain that had remained with her since her parents divorce. But she had always left the thought of divorce up to Tony, considering the fact that he had to endure a dysfunctional marriage and persistent heartaches for his son's sake. Kerri had admired Tony's sensitivity to Fabio, and felt that it was important for him to solely deal with his marital crisis.

'So how's Joey doing?' she asked him. And Tony spent the next few minutes informing her about his brother's legal situation.

They had really enjoyed each other's company, and Tony had been on his third espresso, while Kerri had also re-ordered a ham and cheese toast, as they continued to talk and laugh. For a moment there, Tony had felt very happy chatting to Kerri, forgetting about his family worries, and his early confrontation with Consuela.

CHAPTER NINE

Two weeks later, the family attorney contacted Tony at the office, to sadly inform him that his parents were returning that day home, without Joey. He explained to him that the judge had not granted his bail, due to the serious nature of Joe's charges. And the attorney felt that an appeal for bail was useless. Firstly, he explained to Tony that Joe needed to provide outstanding exceptional circumstances for bail to succeed. And secondly, the attorney felt that applying for an appeal for bail was going to take several weeks, even months, and that Joe's trial was way due before then. After having put down the receiver, Tony looked up, and found Consuela standing alone at the door, staring at him.

Where's Fabio? Is something wrong?' Tony was quick to ask. He had assumed something bad had happened to Fabio. He thought it was unlikely for Consuela to drop by the office alone, late afternoon, as this was usually around the time Fabio tended to have his daily naps. And Tony knew that Consuela would never have left Fabio sleeping alone in the house.

'Relax. Fabio is playing with his aunt Dina', Consuela answered.

'I hope your not here to make another scene? I have clients coming soon.' Tony was quick to defend himself, as he calmly looked through the business reports in his hand. He thought he better be stern with Consuela, as he didn't know what to expect from her. They hadn't talked to each other since their last confrontation two weeks ago.

'No. Rest assure that I'm not here to make a scene, but to simply tell you that there will be an additional member to our family.'

'What do you mean? Are you pregnant?' Tony

shockingly asked.

'Yes. I'm a few days pregnant. I just thought I would tell you. I only found out from the doctor's today.' Consuela said, showing no emotion. And Tony also showed no emotional response to the news. As far as they were both concerned, it was just another thing to share on their marital agenda.

Tony always hoped that he wouldn't have to go through another pregnancy with Consuela. Not until he had time to slow down from family and business affairs, in order to compromise his position in the marriage. Besides, Tony thought Consuela's pregnancy was odd with the little time they had spent together in bed. But he had recalled, the odd moments here and there, when Consuela had relied on morning stiffness, and catching him off guard. It was those moments that Tony had only felt subdued and powerless to casual sex with Consuela.

'Well! Don't rush to pull out the wine glasses'. Consuela sarcastically said. And Tony stood looking at her with great spite. One of the receptionists had entered the office to ask them if they wanted some coffee, and they both had declined the offer.

'Well! How did you expect me to react? I mean we both know that our marriage has never been on stable grounds. There has hardly been any form of emotional communication between us over the years'; he paused for a few seconds staring at her, 'Besides this pregnancy thing comes as unexpected news for me. I mean it comes at an inappropriate time amidst family concerns and business affairs.' And without a word, Consuela had left his office. She did not even bother to dignify herself with an answer. She could not comprehend why Tony's family and business had both been constant priorities to his own marital family.

It was moments like these, after having flawless

conversations with Tony, that Consuela would turn to booze and hot gossip on the internet, where she would drift off into another world away from her marital problems. And she had always been amazed that she had not turned into an alcoholic over the years. After her brawls with Tony, Consuela had always turned to a bottle of Chardonnay and chatted with different men on the net. She had often talked dirty with them, and even participated in cyber sex, without any conscious thoughts, but it was the sheer nympho pleasure that helped to release her from her empty marital life. After many of her female companions had either found work, went overseas, or got married, Consuela had become the lonely housewife. And her shopping sprees had no longer provided her with a joyful fix, as she had turned her home into a warehouse. But in the past few months, Consuela had found solace in her drinking and internet habit.

Tony was quick to contact Dina to tell her the bad news about Joey. He suggested that they cheer up for their folks sake. Tony told Dina to organize a family dinner tonight to help preoccupy her mind from sad thoughts. And he told her that he would tell Nunzio about dinner at their next work meeting. Late that afternoon, Sylvana and Dominic had arrived back at the estate, after having visited Joe in Santa Monica. They entered the estate, and came in contact with Dina assisting the maid in setting the table. Dina looked gorgeous in a white fashionable sweater, with its fur collar hanging down her chest, and a matching black pants. She had straightened her hair down her back, and had earlier cut her side fringe at Le Femme Coiffeur. And her clothes were matched with a glittering set of diamond stud jewelery.

Dina stood for a few moments staring at her parents with great sadness, and fighting back the tears that had overwhelmed her eyes. She could see that her parents' health had been affected by Joey's ordeal. Dina could see that her mother had lost a lot of weight, and had developed more wrinkles around her cheeks and neck. And Dominic had seemed very pale, with big grey saggy bags beneath his eyes. She ran up to her mother, and tightly embraced her as they both heavily sobbed. Dominic tried to comfort them with a tear drop in the corner of his eye.

'Where's your brother Tony, Ballerina?' Dominic sadly spoke.

'He'll soon be here with Nunzio for dinner.' Dina said, as she used both hands to wipe her tears. 'Why don't you and Mama go upstairs and change clothes. Dinner will be ready in a few minutes', she added with a grin. Dominic put his arms around Sylvana as they both made their way up the staircase. And Dina could see how heartbroken they were. She knew not to expect a lively atmosphere at the dinner table. The whole family was pretty distraught about Joe not being granted bail.

Early that evening, Tony and Nunzio accompanied Dina and her parents for what seemed to be a silent, somewhat impractical, dinner. But as the family had momentously passed the main meal, the tense atmosphere around the table, had begun to ease off a little. Tony sat at the corner of the table quietly updating his father on business, and Sylvana was softly speaking with Dina about Joe's bail hearing earlier that day. And Nunzio stood beside them, admiring some of the dining's antique, sipping on dry white wine. He felt relieved that Joe had not mentioned anything to the family about his advice on China town. He figured that Joe had been more concerned with Sui Lee's truck and the legal ramification of this whole incident.

By this time two housemaids had entered the dining

area, each holding a tray of Panettone cake for dessert. They had all begun to eat dessert, when one of the maids had returned looking very terrified and her whole body trembling.

'What's the matter, Thea?' Dominic asked. Thea was the youngest maid at the estate.

'There's. There's. Sir. There's lots of them.' she found it difficult to breathe, and hardly made any sense to them.

'What are you talking about?' Dominic curiously asked. And the maid had just pointed towards the kitchen, with wide brown eyes, and her uniform apron remained trembling from her great fear.

'What's happened in the kitchen?' Tony curiously stated, and got up to follow his father, as the rest of the family had all soon made their way into the kitchen.

'There seems to be nothing here.' Dina worriedly commented.

'Where's the lots of them?' Dominic asked, as he grabbed Thea's hands in an attempt to comfort her. But she escorted him to the kitchen's side door, and opened it. To the family's horrific shock, there were hundreds of tiny black scorpions crawling out of the two large metal dumpsters. Both Sylvana and Dina screamed, and used their hands to cover their mouths. While the men remained silently still staring at the mass of tiny scorpions embedded across the garden floors.

'What the hell is the meaning of this?' Tony angrily said, kicking a tiny scorpion of his shoe.

'Who is doing this to us?' Dina screamed, clutching onto the top of her head, and began to sob in Nunzio's arms.

'Call the Police, and let them know about this', Nunzio turned to Tony. 'Don't worry Dominic. I'm sure the Police will resolve these trivial games sooner or later.' Nunzio said, as he continued to gently comfort

Dina in his arms. Sylvana could see that Dominic had seemed very pale from the incident, and asked Dina to assist her in taking him up to his room.

Nunzio had later joined Tony who was completing a full statement with Police in the back garden. He could see Police rescue teams loading the tiny scorpions into special crates.

'What do they do with all these things?' Nunzio asked the inspector, as he lit a cigarette.

'Well! I guess after they've been examined, they'll probably be dumped off the sea coast.'

'I didn't know you smoked, Nunz', Tony said, turning towards them.

'Ah! Only in times like these. When I feel a little unsettled, I tend to strike a light.' Nunzio replied, taking a drag from his cigarette.

'How's the family doing back in there?'

'They're fine. Dominic's resting in his room, and Sylvana is comforting Dina in the lounge', Nunzio said, 'She sure didn't take things all that well, tonight.'

'I would say with Joe not making bail, the quiet dinner, and then this had really got Dina stressed out.' Tony could only think of these three reasons to explain Dina's stress.

CHAPTER TEN

Several weeks later Dominic decided to take work leave for health reasons, leaving Tony amidst a pile of business schedules, and more restless brawls with Consuela. The Police were yet to provide the family with a conclusive story about the tiny black scorpions. Sylvana was nursing Dominic's ill health, which doctors related to family stress. Dominic felt weak and Sylvana followed him around the estate with hot soup and medication. She had especially kept a close eye on him this week, because Joe's trial was coming up in three days. Sylvana was anxiously awaiting Joe's trial, and Gino's safe return from Youth camp the following weekend. At times, she left one of the maids to nurse Dominic, while she prayed for the family at Sunday mass.

Dina could no longer help out with family affairs; as she was too busy settling in with Nunzio into their new cottage house in Bel Air. She sorely missed being close to the family, and felt elated by her father's surprise about the cottage over a family dinner two weeks ago. Dina was anxiously awaiting a reply from a job interview she had attended last week at an adolescent counseling centre. And Nunzio was also left to share Tony's burden of business reports back at the company. Later that day, Dina received a call from the counseling centre, informing her that she had been given one of the therapists position at the centre, and that she was to start work in two days. She had quickly hung up, and ecstatically dialed Nunzio back at the office. And she felt a little distressed by Nunzio's lack of interest in the job offer. But Dina decided to shrug it off as one of Nunzio's weird personality lapse. At times she had felt bedazzled by his odd behaviours, and dismissed them as perhaps relating to his past secrets.

Three days later, Tony stopped by the estate before heading down to Joe's trial in Santa Monica. He wanted to check on his father, and to get him to sign some business papers before he had left. Dina was now busy working for the adolescent counseling centre, and could not go with him. Although Dina would have loved to be present for her brother's trial, but it was also her first busy day at the centre, and she would have compromised her position if she was to ask for leave. Sylvana wanted to go with Tony, but he had talked her into staying with Dominic and Gino. He felt that both of them needed her, especially Gino, who seemed to be very distressed over Joey, ever since he had come back from his Canadian trip. Nunzio was busy taking care of things back at the company, while Tony was away. And Bruno was now managing the family restaurant, after Dominic had paid off all the finances, and offered Bruno a reasonable salary.

A few hours later, Tony had arrived in Santa Monica. Joe had walked into the courtroom in a brown suit that Sylvana had brought him at her last visit, especially for the trial. He had lowered his gaze, from his brother and the family's attorney, feeling very ashamed of himself. He also happened to make quick eye contact with Nicole, and what seemed to be her father sitting beside her. Joe felt startled about Nicole showing up at the trial, especially her father. He thought Nicole must have told him about them and the baby, and he had come to accept it. He had hoped to see Dina or Sylvana beside Tony, but thought that they must have had important family affairs to attend to. He had hoped that his father was in good health, as Sylvana had regularly informed him over the phone that Dominic was doing well. Although, he wasn't sure if Sylvana was only telling him this, so that he wouldn't worry about his father while in custody.

Tony felt very disappointed in his brother Joe, and had only attended the trial for his parents' sake. He felt Joey had done a very dumb thing, and that there was no need for the family to go through the entire trauma because of his childish behaviour. Tony had felt very ashamed and angry about the family's surname being read out at the initial arraignment, and hoped that Joe was very satisfied with this social predicament. After all Tony shared similar views to his father's, that Joe was a predicament to the family, and had always been in the past.

It had now been two hours into the court hearing, and the prosecution was sounding very tough on Joey's defense. The family attorney was finding it difficult to defend Joe's access to the truck, and to persuade the jury that Joe was unaware of narcotic substances found in it. It was certainly not looking good for Joe, and Tony could very well sense the tense atmosphere. He had prayed that everything would go well, and more so for his parents sake, than Joey's. He felt Joe had done a foolish thing, and that he did not deserve his full sympathy. He wondered when Joe was ever going to grow up and act his age. Nicole had anxiously maintained to make eye contact with Joe, as the prosecution called an FBI agent into the witness box, and her father remained stern as he kept his eyes focused on the judge. The prosecution was certainly out for blood and justice, and kept reinforcing to the judge and jury the substantial evidence that was pending on Joe. After the defense had cross examined the FBI agent, the judge had called for a thirty minute recess, to allow some time for jurors to digest the arguments presented by both legal parties.

During recess break Nicole had introduced her father to Tony and the attorney who stood talking beside Joe. It took Tony a little while to realize that

Nicole had been the one Joe was secretly seeing away from the family. And he was surprised to realize that she was unlike how his mother had made her out to be. He had found Nicole to be a warm and affectionate person, and although he had looked out for the tartish flare in Nicole during their conversation, he could not find it. Tony had respected the fact that Nicole had introduced herself in a very diplomatic manner. He had also shared common interests in her father's business ventures. Tony was not the only one shocked by Nicole's lady-like manner, but so was Joe. He was very shocked by Nicole's behaviour, and wondered for a second, if that was really her, or whether she had acted differently in front of her father. He felt that perhaps aliens had abducted the old Nicole, and replaced her with a new one.

Joe enjoyed talking to Nicole's father. He had only seen a photo of Warren back at Nicole's apartment. And he was surprised by Warren's visit. Joe had never felt like this around Nicole before. She was just a flawless girlfriend who he used for casual sex. Joe couldn't understand these strange sensations, and wondered if they had anything to do with love, or simply the fact that he'd been away so long from family and friends. But for now, he was just happy to be around Tony, Nicole and her father. Joe felt very surprised and shocked by her father's casual attitude towards him. It seemed as if they had known each other for quite sometime now. The fact that Tony seemed to be enjoying his conversation and exchanging smiles with them, made Joe wander if there was a chance that Nicole would someday be part of their family. And as he continued to talk to Nicole and her father, the family's attorney had returned, and took Tony away from them for a brief discussion.

The family attorney had informed Tony that the jury

were finding it difficult to believe that Joe had nothing to do with the drug containers, especially when he was caught behind the wheel of the truck. To the family attorney this was the weakest point in their case, because it was difficult to persuade the jury that Joe and the drug containers were two separate issues. This was especially so, when FBI agents had literally raided China town and found no evidence of Sui Lee and the black maze. Shortly after Sui Lee had learnt about Joe's capture, he made sure that he had been long gone from China town. Although some of Sui Lee's men were captured by federal police, it was still difficult for the family's attorney to prove Joe's innocence in court. But he had informed Tony that he would reinforce some of Joe's reasonable points after the break, but the attorney felt that the whole matter lay in the hands of the jury.

Joe, Nicole and her father could see that Tony looked somewhat distressed by what the attorney had to say, as they stood watching opposite to them. Nicole's father walked over to Tony and their attorney, allowing Nicole to spend some time with Joe alone.

'Just hang in there, champ', Nicole said with a grin, as she rubbed both of his hands, and fought the tear that was about to slip from the corner of her eye. 'No matter what happens the twins and I will be here waiting for you.' She assured him, and gave him a gentle kiss on his cheek.

'Twins?' Joe's eyes lit up. 'You mean you're going to have two babies' Nicole nodded with overwhelmed tears and excitement. She had only recently found out that she had been actually carrying two healthy baby girls.

'Wow! I'm going to be a father to two.'

'Two baby girls', Nicole quietly spoke, wiping a tear away.

'Wow! Two bambinos' Joe surprisingly said. It was

95

the first time Joe had felt emotionally in response to Nicole. He was able to appreciate her care, and her true love for him. He had never before intimately comprehended her emotional presence, and strangely enough, he had come to realize that Nicole had been a victim of his ostracized love for quite sometime now. And in a strange way, he had started to feel very sympathetic towards her. Joey felt as though he had provided Nicole with black justice towards her endless love. He had stared very curiously, yet in an innocent way, into her crystal blue eyes, both of them consumed in a moment of love, adrift in a world of their own, about to reach a peak of passion. And Joe could hear, from what seemed to be in the far distant, the court bailiff announcing their return to trial. And without any conscious thoughts, Joey had pulled in Nicole closer to him, giving her a great big passionate kiss, and Nicole had felt totally mesmerized by her total victory of love.

Nicole's father had stepped closer to them, letting out a fake dry cough, and they had all returned to their seats. Both the prosecution and the defense had clearly delivered their closing statements to the jury. And moments later, the courtroom was left in great suspense awaiting the jury to return with a verdict. Joe and Nicole had remained making eye contact with each other, as they anxiously waited the jury's return. Fifteen minutes later the jury had made their way back into the courtroom, and the judge had immediately asked their spokesman as to their decision. And Tony and the attorney, joined by Nicole's father, were sternly staring at the spokesman with great suspense. Joey decided not to face the jury in an attempt to further hold onto his nerves. Rather his eyes remained fixated on Nicole.

The jury had found Joey to be guilty of all accounts, and every one was further shocked by the judge's sentence of six years imprisonment. Joe stood totally stunned and numb in the courtroom, and Nicole let out a merciful cry. Both Tony and the attorney remained in shock for a few seconds, baffled by the judge's decision. Nicole ran up to Joey, crying her eyes out, as he was being escorted away. And the family's attorney stood behind her reassuring him that he was going to appeal against the decision. Tony sat back into the courtroom chair feeling very distressed and somewhat numb from the dreadful outcome of the trial. He just did not know what to tell the family.

CHAPTER ELEVEN

After the trial, Tony continued to have a discussion with Nicole and her father at a small snack bar, opposite the courtroom. Nicole had mentioned to Tony about Joey's twins, and although Tony was further shocked by startling news of the day, he could only offer Nicole his blessings.

'I never really could understand, Joey. He would always get himself into trouble as a kid. I find that he is easily manipulated by others. He's a good kid. He's very generous, and affectionate to the family. But he just doesn't think right', Tony explained to Nicole and her father, holding back his tears. He had after all felt very distressed about his younger brother being imprisoned. 'I don't really know how to explain today's nightmare to the family', Tony looked up helplessly at Nicole.

Nicole's father, Warren, had offered Tony to help out in paying for Joey's appeal trial. Tony was quick to thank him for his generosity. He felt very grateful for Nicole and Warren's moral support and concern. They seemed to be very nice and reasonable people to Tony. Nicole started to cry and hugged her father.

'I think he's a very lucky guy to have someone like you, who cares a great deal about him.' Tony said. He wished he could say the same thing about his wife. But he knew that she had not really loved him as a person, but rather it was a marriage of convenience. Consuela got to respect her father's decision to marry an Italian man, and most of all having to immigrate to America. This had been a long time fantasy for Consuela, who was stuck in a poor Sicilian village with a brutal father, and had hoped for a prince to sweep her away from the village.

After having his last sip of coffee, Tony once again

had thanked Nicole and her father for having attended Joey's trial. They exchanged phone numbers, and Nicole's father was anxious to have another meeting with Tony soon. This time he had hoped it would be over business. Warren felt very subdued and passionate about his business, just like Tony and Dominic. Tony had promised to keep in touch with them back in Beverly Hills, and left.

In reaching the Californian highway, Tony pulled his car into the emergency lane, and sat heavily sobbing like a little lost kid. It had been a very distressing day for Tony, as he didn't expect Joey to be imprisoned. He had felt sorry for him, and most of all for the family. He was still contemplating ways of delivering the bad news to the family. He did not know how his parents were going to react to the news, and held grave concerns about his father's health. He decided it was best to contact Dina first, and to fill her in on the bad news. Tony picked up the receiver of the car phone, and reluctantly dialed Dina's number. He thought he better pull himself together, and to be strong for the family's sake.

'Hello! Hello! Dina.' Tony reluctantly, but sadly spoke, as he laid his head back into the driver's headrest. 'Things didn't go well for Joey. Joey's in a big mess.' Dina was shocked at the other end of the line. She sensed bad news from the sound of Tony's shaky voice.

'Why? What's happened to Joey?' Dina worriedly asked, and she could feel butterflies in her stomach.

'Joey got six years jail.' Dina began to heavily sob.

'Oh! My God. Poor Joey. Oh! My God.'

'Don't worry Sis, our attorney is immediately applying for an appeal.' Tony was quick to reassure her.

'Are they going to keep him in Santa Monica?'

'I'm afraid so, because Joey was charged over there.' Tony sadly said, 'See how you are going to tell Mama and Papa. Perhaps wait until Nunzio gets back from work. I'm on my way home.'

'Well! Since you're coming back home, pass by the estate. Nunzio and I will meet you there. I think it's better that we're all there when Mama and Papa have to hear the news.'

'Okay! See you then. Ciao.' Tony agreed.

Dina had called Nunzio, and explained Joey's situation, and he had agreed to meet her at the estate after work. Dina had half an hour left from work, and she had decided to complete her clients' reports the next day. She had explained to reception that she was leaving early due to family problems, and they could tell from her face that the problems had seemed to be big. After driving towards the estate, Dina had decided to change route, and to pass away time back at the cottage. She felt too nervous to face her parents alone, and wanted to make sure she was there around the same time as Tony and Nunzio. She went straight to her bedroom, and continued to heavily sob like a new born baby. Dina had also worried about how her parents were going to react to Joey's news, considering that both Dominic and Sylvana suffer from hypertension. She had felt enormous sympathy for Joey, and helplessly continued to cry.

Early that evening, Tony had met up with Dina and Nunzio outside the estate, comforting his sister as she cried in his arms. Nunzio felt that it was best for Dina and Tony to inform their parents that Joey had received a two year rather than a six year sentence, until the appeal had been settled. Tony thought that was a good idea considering the health conditions of his parents. Sylvana had anxiously hollowed out to them from the front door. She could see the long faces on all three of them as they made their way towards her. And before Sylvana had said a word, Dina quickly embraced her, and they both cried endlessly in each other's arms. Tony walked passed them, and found his father sitting in the lounge recliner, and his eyes consumed with tears. Tony embraced his father.

'I'm sorry, Papa. I'm so sorry about Joe', he sadly said, and his eyes were also consumed with tears.

Nunzio suggested to the family that they all had to be strong for Joey. He also suggested that their attorney was working on an appeal against the decision. He attempted to comfort Dominic and Sylvana, by telling them that two years imprisonment would not seem to be too long. And reinstated the fact that there was the appeal trial to also consider. By then, they had all been sitting close to each other in the lounge silent, with Sylvana and Dina continuing to softly sob. Their silence was soon interrupted by the maid passing the phone to Dominic.

'Where's Gino?' Nunzio asked.

'He's at Brad's house', Sylvana quietly spoke, sobbing through her words. 'Please, nobody tells Gino the truth. Just tell Gino that his brother's trial is continuing, for now.' Sylvana spoke shortly afterwards.

Tony sensed that his father was receiving some sort of bad news over the phone. He noticed that Dominic had a pale face. He wandered if the phone call had been related to the disturbing parcels that his father had been receiving. Dominic remained mainly quiet throughout the call, with the occasional 'yes' or he simply nodded his head. Tony had become very curious watching his father staring into space with wide open eyes, and his face getting paler by the minute. Dominic had quietly nodded his head towards the end of the call, and put the phone down.

'Who was that Papa?' Tony curiously asked. And

before Dominic had answered, Nunzio had also noticed Dominic's white face.

'What's the matter Dominic? You don't look too well.' Nunzio said, grabbing Sylvana's and Dina's full attention.

'That was the family's attorney. He talked about appealing Joe's case', Dominic sadly said, 'But he says Joe got six years in jail.' Dina looked very shocked, and so did Tony and Nunzio. They hadn't had time to fill in the attorney on their decision.

Sylvana began to heavily sob in Dina's arms. 'It's allright Mama. You'll see the appeal will go fine for Joey.' Dina comforted her. Tony was lost with words, and did not know what to tell his father. He was glad Dina had said something.

'Is there anything else you're hiding from your Mama and I, son?' Dominic looked at Tony.

'No, Papa. We felt it wasn't necessary to say much until the appeal had been settled.' Tony said.

'Perhaps, you and senoira should go upstairs and lye down for a while.' Nunzio suggested, and Dina thought that was a good idea.

Dominic used Sylvana's arm to rest on, as they made their way to the staircase. Dominic's leg had become stiff after taking the first step up the stairs. Soon Sylvana had felt Dominic's whole body stiffen, and his face had turned pale blue. Sylvana screamed for help, and found it difficult to keep a hold of Dominic. Dominic fell backwards onto the floor just beside the staircase, just as Dina, Tony and Nunzio came running towards them. Dina and Sylvana began to panic and cry, and felt helpless, as they watched Dominic experiencing shortness of breath. And Tony stood beside Nunzio very shocked from Dominic's great pain and wide open eyes.

'Call paramedics', Nunzio said to Dina, as he knelt

102

down and loosened Dominic's tie. He also used his handkerchief to wipe the saliva oozing out from the side of Dominic's mouth.

'Grab me a blanket, senorita.' Nunzio referred to Sylvana.

By then Dominic had lost consciousness, and Nunzio decided to administer CPR, while Tony stood silently terrified by his father's weak condition. He felt guilty about his nerves locking in on him, and his inability to help his father.

'I can't find a pulse', Nunzio looked up at Tony with great shock, 'I need to administer chest compression. I need you to blow into your father's mouth, while I pump the chest.' He added. Dina comforted Sylvana who stood holding a blanket, and they both had endless tears trickling down their face.

'I can feel a pulse now', Nunzio told Tony, as he grabbed the blamket off Sylvana and covered Dominic. The maid had let paramedics through the front entrance, and they had quickly placed an oxygen mask on Dominic and began to get a reading of the heart pulse. Moments later, they had taken Dominic out on the trolley bed, and Sylvana had escorted him in the ambulance, while Nunzio and Dina followed them in Tony's car to the hospital.

CHAPTER TWELVE

A few hours later, the family sat in the interview room, accompanied by Gino and their loyal Italian housemaid. A male nurse had come out of the emergency room to tell the family that the doctor had needed a few more minutes to complete her examination of Dominic, before she could come out and give them an assessment of their father's condition. Sylvana and Dina decided to both visit the hospital's chapel to pray for Dominic's safe recovery. Tony sat silently, staring at the floor, anxiously awaiting news from the doctor. The whole family had been very shaken and upset by tonight's ordeal, especially Tony who had always felt closer to his father than anyone else. They had asked the maid to contact Consuela, and to let her know what had happened that night. He didn't expect Consuela to join them in hospital, as Fabio would be asleep, and it was a bit late to call for a babysitter.

Moments later, Sylvana had returned with Dina, blowing her nose, just as the female Asian doctor had stepped out from the emergency room. Both Nunzio and Tony stood up anxiously to hear what the doctor had to say. The doctor informed them that Dominic had experienced a heat attack that night, and luckily for him, it had not been a fatal one. She paused to thank Nunzio for his CPR response to Dominic back at the estate, as she felt that CPR helped Dominic's breathing to remain stable. She informed Tony and the family that Dominic was at the moment stable, and that she had him on dopamine. She went on to explain that she may need to stick a breathing tube down his throat should Dominic fall into coma. But the doctor was quick to reassure them that his heart pulse and blood pressure were at the moment satisfactory. Tony had asked if Dominic was up to visitors, and the doctor had agreed to allow two visitors at a time. Tony and Sylvana had decided to go and see Dominic first. And the doctor had escorted them back into the emergency room, explaining to them that Dominic had a tube stuck in his neck to help her get a quicker reading of the blood flow to the heart.

Tony and Sylvana had nervously entered cubicle four, not expecting to see Dominic with all sorts of tubes stuck into his body. Sylvana and Tony gently held onto his hands, and Dominic kept opening and shutting his eyes tiredly, but aware of their presence in the room.

'You gave us quite a scare tonight, Papa', Tony smiled, and Sylvana looked at Dominic with great anticipation, and her eyes consumed with tears. Dominic tiredly nodded his head to indicate that he had comprehended their presence with him.

'The doctors say you're going to be fine, sweetheart', Sylvana smiled, gently swiping her hand across his forehead.

'Get some rest, Papa. We'd better go so that Dina and everyone could see you.' Tony said.

'Don't worry sweetheart, we'll be right outside.' Sylvana assured him, giving him a gentle kiss on the forehead, before having left with Tony. Tony had spotted his father's doctor at the nurse station on their way out.

'So what happens to my father now, doctor?' he asked.

'Well! I would like to keep your father here for a few hours, just until I've checked all the blood results, and then he'll most likely be taken to coronary care unit for a close monitoring of the patient's heart function.' The doctor said, before being hurriedly whisked away by two registered nurses to what seemed to be another emergency.

That night Sylvana stayed by Dominic's bedside, while everyone else went home to rest. Around two a.m. an orderly came and took Dominic up to C.C.U, and Sylvana went with them. Early next morning, Dina and Nunzio visited Dominic before going to work. Dina had brought her mother a toasted sandwich, orange juice, and her blood pressure pill.

'Howse Papa doing, Ma? Dina asked.

'He's doing well. He's still sleeping', Sylvana tiredly spoke, as she took the bag from Dina. 'The doctor says that your father is making a slow, yet satisfactory recovery. He said your father might be able to go home in two days. They're just waiting for the heart pulse to go a bit higher.'

'You look very tired, Mama. After work, I'll come and stay with Papa, while you go home and have a rest.' Dina said.

'It's okay. I'll be fine. Tonight, I'll go home and sleep. Where are your brothers, Ballerina?'

'Gino will be coming soon with one of the maids, possibly Thea. And Tony called me this morning to say that he'll come visit Papa later this afternoon. Nunzio is in the visitors' lounge, if you want to come and see him. He also thought he'll drop by to check on Papa before going to work.'

'Oh! Yes, of course, I want to see Nunzio. I still have to thank him for what he did for your father last night.' And they both headed down the corridor towards the visitors' lounge.

Meanwhile, back at the office, Tony was confiding in Kerri about Joe's trial and his father's cardiac arrest. He had enjoyed sharing his family affairs with Kerri, and she had always been an excellent mentor. Tony wished he could share his stress and anxiety with Consuela, but his feelings had only naturally spurted

106

out around Kerri.

'You know, I'm so worried about Papa, that I seem to be having a lot of trouble concentrating on work issues', Tony said to Kerri, as they both shared the two setter sofa in the office corner.

'Just hang in there. It's natural not to feel your usual self, considering all the things that have been happening in your family. You're under a lot of stress'. Kerri comforted him, rubbing her hand up and down his right arm.

'You know, I got to meet Joe's girlfriend Nicole, yesterday at the hearing. And she seemed nothing like what my mother had described her to be. She actually seemed like a very nice person, who cared a great deal about Joe.'

'Well sometimes we tend to judge people from our first encounter with them, but we later discover that they are quite different as to our initial meeting with them. And perhaps that's what happened with your mother and Nicole.'

'Perhaps you're right. Well we have to give her the benefit of doubt, considering that I'm going to be an uncle soon to twins.' They both laughed. 'You know I've only told you so far about Joe's twins. I still have to tell the family. But, of course, I don't want Papa to know until way later down the track.'

'How's things with you and Consuela?', Kerri asked him.

'Still the same. We hardly talk to each other anymore. We only exchange the odd word, here and there. I come home, play with Fabio, pre-heat dinner in the microwave, watch a bit of Teley or read the business journal, and later crash in bed. Consuela always seems to be locked in the den, glued to the internet.'

'I can really see she shares your family stress', she

smiled.

'Well the only family Consuela relates to is a huge cauldron and a broomstick.' They both endlessly laughed. And moments later found themselves up close staring into each other's eyes, contemplating whether or not they should kiss.

Although Kerri had been Tony's best friend for a long time, he had lately been thinking about her from a different perspective. He had grown more fond of Kerri in the past three months, and had experienced different sorts of feelings whenever he was around her. He could see that he was enjoying time with her more than before. And he was aware of the number of times he had come looking for her to share his family problems. It seemed that they were both on the same communication wave. They could see the tiny spark in each other's pupils that indicated two burdened souls that were yearning for real passion. But their moment of happiness was shortly interrupted by a knock on the door. They had both blushed and felt a little awkward, as Tony suggested that he better see who's at the door. It was Tony's nine-thirty a.m. appointment with five Japanese entrepreneurs.

CHAPTER THIRTEEN

Later that afternoon, Sylvana was assisting Dominic in having some hot soup. She was glad to see her husband sitting up, talking and laughing and without a pale face. The nurse had entered the room to check Dominic's chart book, and to take his blood pressure. And when she had left, Tony had arrived with a giant bouquet of yellow tulips, and a box of chocolate.

'You shouldn't have troubled yourself, son', Dominic said.

'It's no trouble, Papa. How are you feeling?'

'Fit like a horse, thank God.' Dominic said cheerfully, and both Sylvana and Tony smiled.

'What did the doctor's say, Mama?' Tony turned to Sylvana.

'They said your Papa's condition is improving, and they are just waiting for his heart pulse to increase a little higher, before we can take him home', she said with a smile.

'That's good to hear. So what's been happening? Who has come to visit Papa today?' Tony asked his mother.

'Oh! Lots of people. Your father had lots of friends visit him, today.'

'Did Consuela bring over Fabio to see Papa?' Tony reluctantly asked. He wasn't sure whether Consuela would come or not, considering what's going on between them.

'Yes, she came around the same time Gino was here. Those red roses are from her.' Sylvana pointed to the white ceramic vase on the shelf.

'Don't you need to get some sleep, Mama?' Tony had noticed his mother's blood-shot eyes.

'Don't worry son. Since your father is doing well, tonight I will go home with Dina, and come back tomorrow morning.'

The nurse had re-entered the room to tell Sylvana that there was a visitor for the family waiting in the visitors lounge. Sylvana had gone to see who it was, followed by Tony. Sylvana was soon to discover that behind the enormous bouquet of coloured flowers stood Nicole with a smile. She had permed her blonde hair, and let it hang down her back. She wore a long white mink coat, which had covered most of her tall, slim figure. And her sparkling white gold jewelery made her seem like a very attractive high class woman. Even Tony looked very impressed with Nicole, standing behind his mother.

'Hello! Senorita. These are for your husband. I am happy to hear that he is making a speedy recovery.' Nicole said with a smile, reaching out the floral bouquet to Sylvana. And before Sylvana had a chance to respond, Tony had quickly stepped forward from behind his mother to greet her.

'Hi! Nicole. You shouldn't have troubled yourself. How's your father?' Tony asked.

'He's fine. He sends his warmest wishes to the family. He was tied back with work meetings, and couldn't come along with me.'

Sylvana stood silent and stunned by Nicole's presence. She felt Nicole had a lot of nerves coming to visit Dominic in hospital. Sylvana had thought it was neither the right time nor place to make a scene. Although she had respected the fact that Nicole had not entered Dominic's room. Her husband was certainly in no condition to learn about Joe's secret lover.

'Nicole, why don't you go down to the cafeteria, and order us three espressos. Mama and I will be down shortly.' Tony said, placing a twenty dollar note in Nicole's hand. He had hoped to avoid a confrontation between Sylvana and Nicole. Besides, Tony felt he needed a few moments to explain things to his mother.

Nicole had caught on to Tony's thoughts, as she had not felt totally comfortable around Sylvana. Tony turned to his mother, as Nicole had made her way to the lifts.

'Now Mama, I know you don't approve of Nicole. But I also do not want to see your blood pressure shoot high.' He could tell that his mother was hardly pleased to see Nicole through her facial expressions.

'How do you know her? Nicole. Whatever her name is.' Sylvana sounded spiteful, and looked very unhappy.

'I met Nicole and her father at Joe's trial.' Tony explained to his mother that Nicole seemed to be a different person, and that she had really cared about Joe. He also told her about Nicole's father offering to pay Joe's legal expenses. Sylvana still remained unsympathetic towards Nicole, but had slightly appreciated their great concern for her son. And she knew that if there was a slim chance of accepting Nicole, well it was going to take quite some time. She wasn't sure if Dominic would accept her at all.

Nonetheless, Tony had convinced Sylvana to at least join them over a cup of espresso. Tony thought it was still early to tell his mother about Joey's twins. First, he wanted his mother to get to know the other side of Nicole. The gentle and caring side that is.

'I'll just check up on your father, and join you later', Sylvana quietly spoke. Tony rushed down to the cafeteria to tell Nicole that it was too early to say anything about the twins. He told her that she needed to slowly ease herself into his family, and that occasional dinners were a good start. Tony also offered to take her father's business card to get to know him better. As business work was Tony's best social skill and forte.

'You know Tony; I totally understand where you

and your family are coming from. And I respect the family's honour, tradition and position in the Italian community. I guess it was difficult for me to understand Joe's background, until recently. I mean, we totally had a different family upbringing. I had always felt lonely growing up as a child with two busy working parents. And this had led me to feel totally alone and envious of other families. I grew up questioning my self-worth and needs. The only thing I totally understood was my feelings towards Joey. I really do love him. And I guess coming to understand my own character more better had come from many years of therapy, and in recent months my father treating me as a priority to business, and not the other way around.' Nicole sadly said.

'I'm sorry that you had to go through some pretty rough times growing up as a kid.' Tony sympathetically said. She looked up to him and smiled.

'I want to thank you for your understanding. I'm sure Joey's mother must have painted an ugly picture of me. I regret ever stepping foot at the estate. I hope that someday Sylvana will forgive me.' She looked helplessly towards Tony.

'I'm sure she will. Just give her some time', He assured her.

Sylvana quietly joined them at the table, and took a sip of her cold espresso.

'Would you like me to order you another espresso, senorita.' Nicole offered.

'No thank you. I'm right.' Sylvana answered, hardly making eye contact with Nicole.

'So what's your father's business all about?' Tony asked Nicole.

'He owns a major distribution company which is connected to smaller business franchises, selling security alarm systems to both domestic and commercial properties', Nicole replied with a smile, reaching out to the basket beside her, that she had earlier grabbed from the car, before ordering the three espressos.

'I've brought you some chicken fettuccine and chocolate profiteroles, senorita. I thought you might be feeling a little hungry.' Nicole offered Sylvana the small basket, and Sylvana reluctantly accepted it from her, after having initially glanced at Tony.

Tony took the food out of the basket and shared a profiterole with his mother. And Nicole had explained to them how her father had shared reserved feelings about her seeing Joey in the past. But that he had come to accept Joey recently because of his daughter's great admiration of him. Nicole also explained to Tony and Sylvana that her father had helped her to change into becoming a different person, who was much calmer and appreciative of other people.

'You know, my father said that if I was ever to become a close friend of the Abrucci family, that it was important for me to totally change into a much calmer and accepting person. Apparently, he knew a couple of Dominic's business associates, who had highly spoken of your family. My father said that you were a close-knit family who had shared power and success, and most importantly traditionalist values. And my father felt that if ever I was to become a close friend of the Abrucci's, then I really had to change my social attitude, and to become a high class noble character who had felt emotionally drawn to other people.' Nicole said. She put on a diplomatic front around Sylvana, and was very selective in her choice of words. She did not wish to spell out the fact that she was spellbound and madly in love with Joe, in order to maintain a harmonious connection with Sylvana.

'Your father sounds like a very wise man, who

113

carries some of his own important social ideals.' Tony said, and Sylvana took a quick glance of the two of them, before returning to mashing her half of the profiterole.

Tony had noticed that his mother was not saying much, and was quick to suggest that she'd take some profiteroles up to his father.

'I'd better get going. I'm meeting my father for dinner tonight.' Nicole said as she stood up, grabbing a hold of her white handbag.

'Well perhaps you and your father can join us for a family dinner after Papa is discharged from the hospital.' Tony offered, passing her the empty basket.

'I would really like that.' Nicole smiled, and turned to Sylvana, 'Caio senorita', and left.

CHAPTER FOURTEEN

Several weeks had passed, and Dominic was making a healthy recovery back home, after having a physio visit him regularly to help him with his medical aftermath of occasional migraines and tense shoulder and neck nerves. The family doctor had also been paying Dominic weekly visits to monitor his high blood pressure, and alter his medication dose. Dominic seemed in good spirits to the family, but his diagnosis indicated that he was still a little weak, as it was difficult for the doctor to regulate his blood pressure. Dominic had been looking forward to returning to the company, and had spent the past few days arguing with Sylvana and Tony about it. Sylvana found it difficult to persuade Dominic to retire from work. He was adamant about maintaining his position in the company, as long as he felt healthy and sane.

It was a bright sunny day in Bel Air with a light cool breeze passing across the cottage veranda. There stood Nunzio half naked against the rails with the light breeze ruffling through the top of his hair. From inside the bedroom, Dina sat up naked under the bed sheets, once again disappointed with Nunzio's love making. It was quick sex, no foreplay, and it had left Dina feeling dissatisfied. She had yearned for her husband to fulfill her intimate passionate desires, but was soon beginning to give up, and to redirect all her desires towards healing adolescents in crises. She stared at her husband's back, and wandered if his hopeless love making had any relation to his secret past. She thought that one day soon she was going to confront him about their dysfunctional sex life.

Dina covered herself with a white satin robe, and made her way towards Nunzio. She put her arms around him, and gave him a gentle kiss on the shoulder.

115

He continued to silently stare across the pastures views that lay ahead of him. And as usual he showed no affection whatsoever.

'What are you thinking about sweetie?' Dina said, once again feeling that she had to instigate a conversation whenever Nunzio seemed to be in another world.

'I was thinking about Dominic', he turned to her.

'Oh! Papa. Why?' She sounded startled.

'Well! I was thinking that your father had been cooped up at the estate feeling ill and depressed for so long now.'

'But it's only natural, considering all the family problems and his health.' Dina was quick to interrupt.

'I know that. But being at the estate the whole time will only make your father think about Joe and this will only tend to make your father more sick.'

'But the doctor said he's still a little frail. What are you suggesting?' Dina said, looking at him with great curiosity.

'But your father seems to have made a good recovery, and besides he's taking medication for his blood pressure. I just got this idea, after learning from Tony about a deserted family cabin at Bazrock Bay.'

'Oh! I know. It's been years since anyone in the family has been up there. From what I can recall no one has been there, ever since Joey used to go fishing up there with his college friends.'

'Well! I thought that perhaps I could take Dominic fishing there this weekend.'

'Oh! I don't know, honey. Isn't it early for my dad to be doing such outdoor activities. Besides I don't know if Mama will let him go.'

'Well! We'll just have to convince her, for your father's sake, babe', Nunzio put his arms around her; 'There is nothing stressful about it. It will do Dominic a lot of good to spend some time away from the estate in a quiet and serene place. He'll enjoy re-visiting his old tackles and fishing rods, and it will be just a man to man thing, just for the weekend.' He smiled.

'I don't know. I mean it sounds like a good idea, but you would have to convince Mama of it.' Dina said and seemed to be a little worried about her father.

'Well! If it's just your mother you're worried about, then I'll have a word with her.' Nunzio seemed a lot more cheerful as he went back inside to take a shower.

Over the next three days, Nunzio had convinced Sylvana that her husband needed a short trip get away. Besides, Nunzio had convinced her that the trip would help Dominic to unwind from the strange parcels he'd been receiving in the past week, and to take his mind of Joe's appeal trial. Sylvana had finally given in to the thought that perhaps Dominic had needed to clear his mind through a fresh breath of air. Besides, Sylvana thought the trip was for two days, Dominic's medication would be beside him, and of course he had Nunzio beside him should he require CPR.

Late Friday afternoon, Sylvana and Dina had waved goodbye to Dominic and Nunzio as they sailed off in a small cruise boat from the Californian pier. They first made plans to stop by the cabin and to unload some of their stuff, before spending Friday night fishing in the sea. That night Dominic felt totally relaxed by the peace, the sea's aroma and the moonlight presence as he dipped his rod into the sea. He closed his eyes and with a wide grin enjoyed taking some deep breaths from the light cold sea breeze that kept gushing across his face.

'You know Nunzio. I'm already enjoying this trip. I feel very relaxed. I can't remember the last time I went fishing. I think last time was when Tony was a little boy. You know my father was a fisherman in Sicily when I was a young boy, and I vaguely remember spending some times with him on the boat.' Dominic said cheerfully.

'I'm glad to hear you're feeling more relaxed. You seemed a bit tense back at the estate.' Nunzio spoke as he reeled a small salmon in.

'You seem to be catching more salmon than me', Dominic turned to the fish basket.

'Oh! It's just my lucky night, Dominic.'

Later that evening, Nunzio used the cabin stove to cook the fish. He first had to clear all the dust to get the gas to light up. The family had not used the cabin in quite a while, and this was evident from some of the cobwebs that hung low from the ceiling.

'There is nothing tastier than fresh salmon. I love its smell.' Dominic said, enjoying his dinner.

'How about a game of backgammon over a couple of beers, before we call it quits for the night?' Nunzio suggested, and Dominic accepted the offer whole heartedly.

The next morning, Dominic sat fishing outside the cabin's dock beside the lake, while Nunzio remained inside checking through next week's office reports that he had brought with him. Around midday Nunzio stepped outside to let Dominic know that he was going to heat up a few cans of vegetable soup for the two of them, and Dominic accepted by nodding his head, as he was too busy reeling in a large stingray.

'Hey! Dominic. Dominic', Nunzio shouted from the cabin window, 'I thought I'll just set the boat ready for sail, while the soup is simmering.'

'Okay! Nunz.' Dominic raised his hand to indicate that he had also heard him. And moments later Nunzio had returned standing behind Dominic holding the soup pot with two bread sticks.

'I thought we'd go out to sea for a while and enjoy a

warm bowl of soup on deck.'

'Good idea. I'll just put the fish inside, and I'll be right behind you.' Dominic said, grabbing a hold of his rod and the fish basket.

Inside the cabin, Dominic went to place his fishing rod inside the coat closet, and accidentally dropped Nunzio's secret safety box from the top shelf with the tip of his rod. The metal durability of the box had made a loud noise in having reached the ground. Dominic turned around and was surprised to see the box. He took it over to the kitchen bench, and had trouble breaking into it with a tiny screw driver.

'Stop it, Pops. Stop it', Nunzio came screaming through the door, and violently snatched the box off Dominic. And Dominic stood quietly, with the tiny screw driver in his hand, looking very shocked by Nunzio's inappropriate behaviour.

'I'm sorry, Dominic. I'm so sorry. I don't know what came over me', Nunzio said, breathing heavily, and holding onto the box very tight. 'I'm sorry I acted like that. I mean seeing you. Seeing you with my personal box. Trying to open it. That box belongs to me and it contains important family airlooms. There are things in there that are very important to me. Things to do with my family's past. I'm sorry.' Nunzio placed his left hand on his forehead and stared down onto the floor. Dominic felt very disappointed by Nunzio's outrage, but if anything, he was the best person to appreciate and understand the value of people's past. Dominic had suspected that the box had more than family heirlooms, but rather past family secrets. But he knew he had to respect Nunzio's position on the matter without treading on his personal boundaries.

'It's okay, son', Dominic gently patted Nunzio on the shoulder; 'Your behaviour had just taken me by surprise.' Dominic said as he left the cabin.

Later on the boat Dominic was having his soup, and Nunzio had his arm resting on the sail's pole as he silently stared into the sea. Dominic kept glancing at Nunzio from time to time, and after several minutes decided to break the tense atmosphere between them.

'Don't you just love the gentle, cool breeze of the sea?'

'Yes, that's one thing I look forward to when I'm sailing', Nunzio turned to Dominic. Dominic began to feel ill. He seemed very pale, and was starting to feel a little drowsy.

'Nunzio. Pass me my medication.' He reached out his hand to him.

'What's wrong, Dominic. You sure don't look too well.' Nunzio coldly remarked, showing no interest in Dominic's ill condition. Dominic started to breathe heavily and felt sharp chest pains. And Nunzio remained calm, staring at Dominic, as he scraped some scales of the fish on the table. Dominic felt very frightened on top of his pain, as he was totally shocked by Nunzio's lack of attention towards his ill health. He stood up and vomited a little into the water, and with great difficulty shuffled his feet around the table to grab a hold of his Nitrolingual spray. Nunzio violently kicked the table away from Dominic, and Dominic fell onto his knees, hitting the deck hard.

'My stomach is very sore. What did you put in my soup?' Dominic found it difficult to speak as he seemed to be in a lot of pain.

'I just mixed some valiums with the soup. What's wrong Dominic, can't you take a bit of pain.' Nunzio bent down close to Dominic's side. Dominic grabbed onto Nunzio's t-shirt, but felt too weak to maintain a hold of it. He was beginning to feel drowsier by the minute.

'Why are you doing this?' Dominic looked into his

eyes with great contempt. And Nunzio had just responded with an evil grin. 'Why are you doing this?' Dominic reinstated screaming into his face. Dominic used his arms to grab a hold of his belly, and began to roll across the deck.

'Is it money, power? What do you want?' Dominic continued to scream at him. Nunzio remained calm and walked up to Dominic, placing his right foot on Dominic's thigh. He stared into Dominic's eyes for a few moments with a wide grin.

'Oh! No, Dominic. It's not about money. It's got to do with revenge', Nunzio grabbed a tight hold of Dominic's head. 'Picture this Dom, Sicily 1955, You're running from the Polizia, and leaving behind Antonio.'

'Oh! My God. What's Antonio got to do with you?' Dominic said, as he coughed, and both Nunzio and he could hear his chest wease.

'Antonio was my father', Nunzio angrily spoke, pushing Dominic's head back onto the deck. Dominic silently looked back at Nunzio with wide open eyes.

'Oh! My God. You're Antonio's son.' He exclaimed. He never felt this terrified in his whole entire life. Dominic lay down on the deck feeling very ill. He was heavily perspiring, and began to experience shortness in breath.

'You left my father behind to be shot by the Polizia', Nunzio screamed into his face, pointing his finger at him. 'You left my father behind to die.'

'I had no choice. You're father's leg was stuck under the mine's rail.' Dominic's eyes were consumed with tears.

'It's your fault. You failed to help another fellow black scorpion. You left my mother and me all alone without a man in the house. You have dishonoured the group. I will never forgive you for my father's death. Never. Do you hear me, Dominic Abrucci?' Nunzio said, holding back his tears.

'Oh! My God. So it was you behind the parcels.'

'Yes, it was me.' Nunzio said with great contempt, and squeezed Dominic's jaws with his right hand. 'I've been waiting so long for this day. I always grew up thinking about meeting you one day and avenging my father's death.'

'But how did you know where to find me.'

'A female member of the group told my mother that she had seen you jump into a boat filled with refugees going to America.' Nunzio said, as he used the carving knife to gently maneuver it across Dominic's chin.

'Oh! No. Please don't do this.' Dominic had slightly sulked.

'Oh! Don't worry I won't kill you. Well not directly anyway. It would be too easy. Oh! No. I'm still not finished with the Abrucci's.'

'Oh! Please don't harm my family. Oh! Please. I beg you', Dominic mercifully pleaded. But Nunzio was not willing to grant Dominic any mercy. He had been waiting years for this day. Nunzio used both arms to lift Dominic off the deck.

'I have a surprise for you', Nunzio angrily spoke dragging Dominic's feet towards the cabin room. He opened the door and pushed Dominic down the few steps with great force.

Dominic screamed from excruciating pain after having hit the floor. By this time he had felt very weak and drowsy. He could feel his chest and arm to be very numb, and found it difficult to breathe. He lifted his head up, and was shockingly horrified by what he had seen. He found Antonio's head preserved in nitric acid in an empty fish tank. Dominic's eyes were very wide open from shock. He then noticed Nunzio opening the ceiling's vent from the upper deck, and found it difficult to see from direct sunlight on his face. And moments later, his blurred vision had showed him, what seemed to be, black circles falling in heavily onto both him and the floor. Dominic had noticed a black circle on his left hand. He took a closer look at it, and was horrified to learn that it was a small black scorpion. He tried to shake it off, but his left arm had become very stiff, and moments later Dominic fell to the ground after having experienced a cardiac arrest.

CHAPTER FIFTEEN

That same afternoon, the police had called the estate to inform the family about Dominic's death. Sylvana and Dina were greatly devastated with grief, and the family doctor had issued them with sedatives to help them get some sleep. Gino found it difficult to release a great volume of tears, and instead kept rolling across his bed from side to side, biting onto his sweater's sleeves from his pain and anguish. He had wished he had a better relationship with his father, so that he could have found it easier to cry. But after all his mother's cries of grief had reminded him that his father had gone from their lives forever. Consuela had gone over to the office to comfort Tony, but found him crying in the arms of his secretary Kerri. And after having silently stared at them from the office door, Consuela left. She had been feeling very tired in the past two days, and she was due to give birth to her baby girl by the end of the week.

Two days later, the Abrucci family stood in total grief, all in black clothes, besides Dominic's grave sight, as Father Murphy delivered the Arbitrary. It was a fine sunny day, and there had been some immediate relatives and business associates present with the family at the cemetery, including Nicole and her father. There was also the special presence of Joey, accompanied by two police officers, which the prison's social worker had successfully arranged for him on such short notice. Nunzio stood very stern staring at Dominic's casket from behind his sunglasses, comforting Dina who silently continued to weep in his arms throughout the funeral. Besides them stood Tony tall, clinging onto his mother who was stricken with great grief, and continued to heavily sob and make sounds as she breathed in air. Consuela and Fabio stood quietly beside them, and so did Tony's secretary Kerri.

In completing his Arbitrary, Father Murphy looked sadly into Tony's eyes, and silently nodded his head, indicating to Tony and Sylvana to come forward first to place their red roses on Dominic's casket. Later on, the family took turns in throwing down a handful of dust as Dominic's casket was being automatically lowered into the grave. This had ended with Gino being wheeled forward by their Italian maid Thea, where both of them had also slowly released a handful of dust at the top edge of the grave site. Sylvana and the rest of the family stood in between two black limousines accepting the condolences of funeral guests. Sylvana had noticed Nicole comforting Joey in her arms, as he uncontrollably sobbed beside the police vehicle. She felt more distressed by Joey's grief, and felt a lot of tears trickle down her face. Her best friend, Sonia, gave her a tight hug, and they both heavily sobbed in each other's arms. And towards the end, Sylvana had noticed Nicole throwing in a red rose into Dominic's grave.

The Abrucci family and some of their funeral guests had later that afternoon returned to the estate for food and drinks. Joey was not allowed to join his family back at the estate, and returned to prison straight after the burial. Through her grief, Sylvana had noticed Nicole and her father to be present at the estate. She was later surprised to see Nicole helping some of the maids to serve guests with fresh food and beverages. Some guests were quietly talking and nibbling on various savories around the estate, but all members of the Abrucci family did not have the appetite for it. They had all sat quietly and sadly in the lounge, accompanied by some guests.

Later, Sylvana had sadly and slowly strolled across the room, and into the kitchen, were she had found Nunzio silently sobbing with his back to her. She gently tapped him on the shoulder, informing him that he was not to blame for Dominic's trip and cardiac arrest, before grabbing a glass of cold water and returning back to the lounge room. She had assumed that Nunzio had probably felt guilty about initiating the trip that led to Dominic's tragic death. But she was wrong. On the contrary, Nunzio felt relieved by Dominic's death. And was glad to learn that the police had accepted Dominic's death as a sudden heart attack. He felt that he had successfully avenged his father's death. Nunzio cried as a result of Sylvana's great grief and emotion earlier in the lounge room which had flooded back memories for Nunzio of his mother being greatly distressed over Antonio's death.

That night Tony sat outside the estate in his blue corvette heavily sobbing like a little kid who had lost his favourite toy. He was sure going to miss discussing business with his father. Tony had shared a close relationship with Dominic, ever since he was a child. And Dominic's departure from the present world had a devastating effect on Tony's emotions. He could never imagine the family to be complete without his father. He knew that the family would have to struggle now even harder to maintain family cohesiveness, seeing that both Dominic and Joe were absent from the family. He turned the ignition on, and glanced at the bottle of Scotch beside him, and decided to share it alone at Hardington Park.

Kerri was getting ready to sleep, ruffling her pillow, and placing her watch onto the bedside drawer, when she heard a knock at the door. She found Tony slanting against the door, with his tie loose, holding an empty bottle of Scotch. He certainly did not look in an impeccable condition, and he still seemed very tall to her. She could see that Tony's face was filled with grief.

'Oh! Tony. Please come in.' She said, taking a hold

of his arm. And she knew he had been heavily drinking from the great stench of alcohol and his body imbalance, as she helped him make his way onto the sofa.

'I didn't feel like going home, and facing Consuela. I just really felt like seeing you. Is that okay? You're not busy are you?' Tony sadly spoke.

'Of course, not. You know you're always welcome. Besides, I was just getting ready for bed.' Kerri softly said, placing her hand onto his.

'I'm going to miss him. I'm going to miss Papa.' Tony cried onto Kerri's shoulder. And she comforted him by stroking her fingers through his hair. 'I guess I shouldn't be a burden on you. I'll just get going.' Tony said, as he stood up with great difficulty.

'No, please stay. You're too drunk to drive. Please, come and lye down.' Kerri took Tony to her bed. She helped him undress, and took his shoes off as he lay flat on the bed. She grabbed some massage oil and began to gently and smoothly rub his back and shoulders. He felt very tense from all the stress, grief and work that he'd been going through in the past forty eight hours. Tony had a big grin on his face, and his eyes closed, as Kerri continued to rub his back.

'I'm surprised you still have time to stay in shape with all the work you do back at the office.' Kerri was impressed by Tony's muscled physique. She was only used to seeing Tony mainly in suits back at work.

Tony slowly turned around to face her, and she could once again see the deep look of intimate passion flare in his eyes. They both stared silently into each other's eyes, and later Tony used his hands to caress her back, maintaining eye contact with her. He could also sense Kerri giving into their mutual entrapment of seduction. She found it difficult to resist Tony's charming flesh in her own bed. She closed her eyes,

127

and let out a silent breath of warm air. And Tony had noticed her blush from her rosy cheeks. He slowly tilted his head up towards her, and gave her a gentle kiss to the lips. It was also a dream come true for Tony. He had been thinking about being personally close with Kerri for a long time now. And especially with the lack of romance he had experienced for years back at home with Consuela, he also did not wish to hold back on this ultimate opportunity. He grabbed Kerri tightly against his chest, giving her a big passionate kiss, and moments later reached out his hand to turn off the side lamp, where they both had felt deeply immersed in a sea of love.

Tony and Kerri had both remained naked in each other's arms until the crack of dawn. And Tony had woken up to the sound of chirping birds, feeling very invigorated and sexually liberated, after having spent half the night making meaningful passionate love to Kerri. He turned to Kerri, who had remained sleeping and gave her a gentle kiss to the lips, and also noticed her face to be filled with delight from the broad grin she had tiredly responded with. Tony felt a little guilty about making love to another woman only hours later after his father's burial, but at the same time found it difficult to comprehend the fact that he was naked with Kerri under her bed sheets. He felt like it was more of a dream than a reality, and felt enormously exhilarated, knowing that he had spent the night with Kerri. He glanced at his mobile screen, and noticed that a message had been left for him. He looked into it, and with great astonishment, realized that Consuela's water had broke two hours ago, and that she had been taken to St. Vincent's maternity ward to give birth to their second family sibling.

'Oh! Shit', Tony screamed as he jumped out of the bed, and looked to see where his pants were.

'What's wrong?' Kerri tiredly asked, as she ruffled her eye lashes and sat up in bed, covering her breasts with the bed sheet.

'Consuela is in labour at St. Vincent's.' Tony said as he buttoned up his shirt. He bent over towards Kerri and softly spoke, 'Thanks for everything. I'll call you later.' He grabbed his tie and shoes, and rushed out the door. Kerri was glad to realize that Tony had seemed pleased being in the same room with her, and had expressed no regrets about last night.

CHAPTER SIXTEEN

Half an hour later, Tony arrived at St. Vincent's Memorial, and realized that Consuela had already given birth to a healthy baby girl. His mother sat beside Consuela holding the baby in her arms.

'Congratulations, son. You have a baby ballerina.' Sylvana smiled. Tony bent over and gave his mother a hug and kissed the baby on her petite hand. He turned to Consuela, who didn't seem very pleased about his late arrival, and gave her a quick kiss on her forehead.

'Where's Fabio?' Tony glanced up at his mother. He knew he probably wouldn't get a response from Consuela.

'He's with his Aunt Dina.'

'I was too upset about Papa. I drank a whole bottle of Scotch, and crashed in my car at Hardington Park.' Tony was quick to put forward an excuse for being absent from his wife's childbirth.

'Oh! Son.' Sylvana sadly placed Tony's head against hers. He took a quick glance at Consuela, who had maintained an angry face. And he couldn't care less if she had bought into his excuse or not. He had been thinking about initiating a divorce with Consuela some time later down the track. He had been battling for years to maintain a marital life with Consuela, but he was beginning to get tired from the constant arguments he had shared with her in the past several months. Besides, they had hardly said a word to each other in the past few weeks. It was a marriage of convenience, one that supported their son and left them both out in the dark.

Tony's mobile began to sound out a musical ring tone, and he used the hospital's staircase to answer it. It turned out to be the family's attorney calling from Santa Monica. Joe's appeal trial had been successful.

His sentence had been reduced from six to two years. Tony returned to Consuela's room with a wide grin on his face. And Sylvana could tell that Tony had some good news to share.

'What is it son?' She could see eyes light up with joy.

'I have two good news to celebrate today', he excitedly commented, and hoped that Kerri was beside him to give her a big kiss. 'Joe's sentence has been reduced to two years.' Tony hugged his mother, and Sylvana cried in his arms feeling very elated by the news. Consuela showed no interest in their joy, and continued to breast feed her baby.

That same night Tony and Sylvana celebrated Joe's reduced sentence over a family dinner at the estate. Dina and Nunzio also shared in the celebration, drinking dry white wine. Tony poured Gino a glass of wine for the special occasion. Moments later, Tony left the happy family and decided to pass by Kerri's apartment on his way home. He brought up with him Fabio, who remained sleeping in his arms after the drive. Kerri was happy to greet them at the door, and told Tony to lay Fabio in the guest room. Tony returned moments later, and sat close beside Kerri on the couch.

'Congratulations on your baby daughter. I called the hospital earlier, and the nurse on duty informed me that Consuela had given birth to a girl.' Kerri said. She felt a little bit guilty about what had happened between them last night. She realized that she had feelings of true love for Tony, but hated the fact that he was a married man. And wondered if she was deceiving herself into believing that there could ever be a future relationship between Tony and her.

'Can I get you something to drink', she offered.

'Just a little bit of Brandy. I had a couple of white wine back at the estate.' Tony said.

131

'So what did you name the baby?' Kerri curiously asked, as she took a hold of the decanter to pour Tony a bit of Brandy.

'We never discussed it much, but Consuela had mentioned the name Daniela once. So we'll probably end up going with that.'

'That's a very pretty name', Kerri smiled, passing him the Brandy. And they both stared into each other's eyes for a few moments.

'Well, I received some good news. Joe's sentence has been reduced to two years.' Tony commented with a grin.

'Oh! That's wonderful news', Kerri sounded ecstatic, and extended her arms towards Tony, but quickly retracted them because of the thought that he was a married man. And Tony seemed worried about her sudden distance from him. He thought that she had been equally pleased with their love making the other night.

Tony hoped that he hadn't damaged the special friendship boundary they had both shared over the years. He thought that perhaps Kerri was having second thoughts about last night. Tony certainly hoped he was wrong. It had only recently occurred to him that he was madly in love with Kerri, and that fact was reinforced through their recent sexual encounter. He felt that he needed to be closer to her to further fulfill his long awaited sexual needs for another woman, especially seeing that woman is Kerri.

'Your whole family must be thrilled to hear that Joe's trial had been a success.' Kerri said.

'You know, it had been a surprise to all of us to hear that Joe's sentence had been reduced. With Papa, and that. We failed to recall that trial's day and time. Mama can't wait to go and see Joe in Santa Monica.'

'I really had a great time last night', Tony blushed.

'I really hope that you felt the same way.' He grabbed both of her hands. And she felt a little awkward and uncomfortable. Kerri did enjoy their intimate love making, but she had hoped that Tony was on the same wave line. She had hoped that Tony was referring to intimacy, and not just casual sex. Although she had felt that Tony had performed quite intimately the other night, delicately exploring her whole body during their love making.

Tony slowly leaned forward to kiss her, but Kerri declined his kiss, gently turning her face away.

'What's wrong?' Tony asked with great astonishment.

'Nothing.' Kerri awkwardly spoke. 'It's just that I'm feeling a little bit guilty. Your being married. And now there's a new baby in your life. But don't get me wrong, I have no regrets about what happened between us the other night.' She quietly said. For a moment there, Tony was starting to worry about Kerri's attitude, and then was pleased to hear that she had no regrets about last night. Fabio started to yell out to his father from the guest room.

'I better go and get Fabio. I have to get up early for work tomorrow. I guess I'll see you at the office.' Tony said, letting go off her hands.

Kerri felt a little sad that perhaps there might have been some misunderstanding about their feelings of love towards each other. Her eyes were consumed with tears, and she sat with her back to Tony, who had returned carrying Fabio half asleep in his arms.

'You know. I'm adamant about divorcing Consuela in the near future.' Tony quietly spoke. And Kerri felt a little relieved to hear him say that. Tony made his way to the front door, and before leaving, he quietly whispered to her. 'I'm sorry Kerri, but I know. I know that I am very madly in love with you. I would like to spend the rest of my life with you. I love you.' Tony gently closed the door behind him. Kerri was elated with immense joy. These were just the right words she had hoped to hear from him. She had shared mutual feelings of love towards Tony as well. And uncontrollably she burst into tears, and ran out to Tony who was putting Fabio into his car seat.

'I love you too, Tony. I have always loved you', she cried, stepping out the front door. Tony looked up to her and couldn't believe what he was hearing. It was a dream come true for him. And with a broad grin he momentarily stood staring back at her. Kerri ran forward, extending her arms towards him. 'I love you, Tony', she cried. And Tony ran up to her, and tightly embraced her, as they smothered each other's mouths and face with kisses.

'I love you, Tony.' Kerri joyfully cried in his arms. And Tony took in a deep breath of sheer intimacy, as he brushed his cheek against hers. He tilted her head back, and with a broad grin, gazed happily into her eyes. And then he smothered her lips with a long romantic kiss, and they spent the next few minutes tightly embracing each other besides his car.

CHAPTER SEVENTEEN

Several weeks had passed, and both Kerri and Tony had continued to reignite their love for one another through their passionate encounters on the rebound. At times, she would accompany Tony to family dinners, without arousing the suspicions of other members. Both Tony and Kerri shared a scuttle relationship, pretending to be good friends in front of family and friends. They thought this was the appropriate thing to do, until Tony had worked out the right moment to discuss the idea of divorce with Consuela.

Tony's busy work schedules with the family's business continued to take up a lot of his time, and his relationship with Consuela was slowly deteriorating. Sylvana and Dina had finally convinced Tony to confront his feelings of grief, and to fully accept that his father had gone. It had only been in the past two days that Sylvana had talked him into getting one of the receptionists to clear his father's office. And naturally he confided in Kerri to take care of this delicate matter.

Nicole had dropped by Tony's office, around four forty five p.m., just as he was getting ready to go home.

'Hello! And what do I owe the pleasure', Tony smiled as he caught a glimpse of Nicole standing in the door way. 'Please, come in', he added holding onto a stack of business faxes.

'I just dropped by for a sec. I hope I'm not interrupting anything.'

'Don't be silly, of course not. I could see your stomach has gone bigger.' Tony commented about her pregnancy.

'Well with twins why wouldn't it. I feel like a huge beach whale.' They both laughed, and Tony offered Nicole a seat.

'I just came to say that I'll be spending more time at

135

our country cottage in Santa Monica with mum. I figured that since Dad is busy with the business proposal you offered him, I'll spend sometime with mum in Santa Monica. Besides I'll get to see Joey a lot.'

'I guess he would have called you to tell you about his appeal being successful.'

'Yes, he called me on that day. He sounded very ecstatic about the news, and I broke down in tears. I haven't seen him this happy in such a long time.' Nicole grabbed a hanky from her handbag to wipe a tear.

'You are coming back to give birth in Beverly Hills, aren't you?' Tony asked.

'Oh! Yes. Besides the twins aren't due until another six weeks. Dad does not want to miss out on my delivery.'

'Well I don't want to miss out on seeing my two nieces. Wow, two nieces, isn't that going to be a special sight. You know you're carrying some Abrucci blood in there. I already feel much attached to them.' Tony said, and kneeled forward towards Nicole. 'I'm going to let you in on a little secret. Mama is already knitting some woolies for the girls. I saw them the other day on her bed. They looked very cool. She's even doing one for my little girl, Daniela. By the way, we still feel bombarded by the truck load of toys you gave us. Thanks for that', he whispered, and smiled.

'That's okay. You're welcome. You're a very sweet man. I'm glad that the twins can look forward to a wonderful uncle', she smiled. She was glad to realize that Sylvana had slowly been accepting her into their family. Sylvana had engaged in small conversations with her in the past several weeks, whenever Tony had insisted on Nicole attending family dinners.

'Would you like me to give you a lift anywhere?'

Tony offered, grabbing a hold of his briefcase.

'Oh! No thank you. That's very kind of you. But my father's chauffeur is waiting for me downstairs.'

'Well then I'll walk down with you.' Tony said, and closed his office door after them.

Tony arrived home that same afternoon, only to find his kids with a nanny and half the furniture gone.

'What's going on?' Tony looked startled at the nanny.

'Your wife told me to give you this letter.' Tony went into the study and took the next ten minutes to read Consuela's letter. He realized that Consuela had decided to dump him and the kids for her Scottish internet lover. They had been chatting via the internet for the past eight months, and it seemed that they had shared similar marital encounters. They were apparently both unhappy and felt that they were the isolated partner in the marriage.

Consuela and her Scottish lover, Shaun, have exchanged photographs via the internet, and have even emailed each other love poems. Consuela had explained to Tony in the letter that she was getting too depressed, and felt that she needed a change in life. She also explained to him in the letter that she had sold some of the house antiques, and had taken a substantial amount of their savings for life security purposes. She told him that she was not interested in the actual house, car or company assets, and had hoped that he would use all his personal finances to raise the kids. She had also informed in the letter, that she had felt adamant about ending the marriage, and that she had no second thoughts about returning to either him or the kids. Tony returned to the nanny and found that she had put both Fabio and Daniela to sleep. He placed a one hundred dollar note into her hand, as she grabbed her coat and left.

Tony was furious with Consuela running off like that without giving him some sort of notice. He started to break and throw about some of the home furniture, fuming with extreme rage. He then stood leaning against the wall staring into space, and tiredly began to slide down against the wall until he had reached the floor. He loosened his tie, and continued to stare into the dark with only dim lights coming from both the lounge room and kitchen opposite him. He was actually relieved that Consuela had moved out of his life, but he felt angry about spending the last ten years with a despicable woman. He never imagined that she would have the heart to dump her kids just like that, especially with Daniela only being a few weeks old. His mobile rang, and Tony tiredly answered it. It turned out to be Kerri back at his father's office.

'You sound very tired. Are you asleep?' Kerri asked.

'No. No. It's just that I came home, and found the kids with a nanny and nearly half the furniture gone. Apparently my adorable wife has dumped me and the kids for her Scottish internet stud.'

'I'm sorry to hear that Tony.'

'Oh! Don't worry about it. I wanted her out of my life very soon anyway. So I guess she did me a favour. But I thought she was a cruel and heartless bitch just to leave her two very young children, just like that.'

'I'm so sorry babe. I'm not sure you need to hear anymore bad news.' Kerri reluctantly said.

'What's the matter? Has anything happened to Mama or the family?' Tony sounded very worried.

'No. Nothing like that', Kerri was quick to reassure him, 'But there just seems to be some descrepency with the company's annual records, and they all seem to relate to Nunzio's work code. Listen, I'll be over in twenty minutes to explain things. Okay!'

'Okay! Ciao gorgeous.'

Tony had called his mother back at the estate to inform her about Consuela. And Sylvana offered to baby sit the kids for him while he attended to company work. Neither Tony nor Sylvana were that affected by Consuela leaving the family. She had never been popular with any member of the family, nor had she shown much affection to Tony's family over the years. But Sylvana felt very disappointed in Consuela, and shared similar views to Tony about Consuela being a heartless person, putting her needs as a priority to the two young children. Tony had also called to explain his marital situation to Dina, and Dina also shared similar feelings and views to Sylvana and Tony. Dina told him that he needed to remarry someone who would be a better caring wife than Consuela.

Tony had thrown hints about Kerri being a better mentor than Consuela during their conversation. But he thought he would explain his true feelings about Kerri to Dina over a black espresso, next time they met at a café during their work break. Besides Kerri was due to arrive at his place any minute now. He told Dina that he will see her at dinner tomorrow night at the estate, and closed his mobile. He reached for Kerri's surprise ring in his jacket's pocket, and opened the gift box. He smiled as he stared at the sparkling diamond ring. Tony had been thinking about dining out soon with Kerri, and presenting the engagement ring to her.

Kerri stood knocking at his front door, and Tony jumped up and placed the ring back in his pocket as he went over to open the door.

'You look like shit', was the first thing Kerri said with a smile. She hugged and kissed him. 'Don't worry about anything, baby. I'll look after the kids for you.'

'Did you know you're the best thing that's ever happened to me?' Tony said, as he laid her down on the

139

carpet, and also decided to join her on the floor. He was so pleased to see Kerri opposite him. He felt elated by her presence. She had never been that close to his problems, and he was glad to be in her company. It seemed that Kerri had somewhat magically wiped his feelings of rage away from him. He started to give her little kisses on the side of her neck.

'Not so quick, champ. There's still the bit of bad news I have to tell you.' Kerri reminded him. And he had totally forgotten about the company's bad news.

'Oh! Yes. I had forgotten about that. So what's up, babe.' They both sat up, and Kerri handed him some company papers.

'The records show that some of the company's finances have been diverted to Italy in the past six months. It seems that they are being deposited into a bank transaction in Sicily. And like I said over the phone, all finance is diverted under Nunzio's work code.' Kerri reluctantly said. She felt embarrassed to mention to Tony that his brother-in-law could be taking extra money from behind the family's back.

'Do me a favour babe. Keep this between me and you.' Tony looked at her with great suspicion, and she could see it in his eyes. 'Tomorrow I'll put a new keyword into the company's assets file.'

'Why don't you get some sleep?' Kerri said.

'Only if you spend the night over here.' Tony smiled.

'I'll make some hot coco, while you get changed.' Kerri blushed.

Later they were both having hot coco in bed. 'You know there's something odd about Nunzio.' Tony looked strangely into Kerri's eyes. 'Ever since Papa passed away, he seems very distant from the whole family. And now this. I wonder what's on Nunzio's mind.'

'Perhaps you're reading too much into it', Kerri suggested, as she laid her head on his chest.

'No. No. There's definitely something wrong. Besides, we don't have any business dealings with anyone in Italy. You know, I'm going to send a private investigator to go over to Sicily and check up on Nunzio's background.' Tony sounded very concerned and serious.

'You're actually very serious about this'; Kerri reinforced what Tony had just said.

'Yes. I'm afraid I am. I would like to know what secret past Nunzio holds back in Sicily.' Tony said, as he gently caressed Kerri's hair.

During the night, Kerri felt a little restless, and she had gently slipped away from Tony's arms, as he remained fast asleep. She made herself another hot coco, and gazed at Tony's children as they lay peacefully sound asleep. She felt very sad that their mother had abandoned them. She pulled the doona up to Fabio's shoulders, and quietly left the room. Kerri snuggled up in Tony's bathrobe, lifting her feet onto the sofa, and silently gazed at the mute T.V. She had thought about having to raise Tony's children, once they had exchanged their wedding vows. And she felt she could raise them as if they were her own. Kerri did not mind Tony's children because she was madly in love with him and had totally accepted anything that was a part of him. Besides she felt Fabio and Daniela were very adorable kids. And she could never imagine as to why Consuela had decided to abandon her beautiful family. She was certainly going to stick to Tony like bees and honey. She couldn't imagine life without him.

Tony had certainly filled a big empty gap in Kerri's life, and she was looking forward to sharing the Abrucci's family cohesiveness. It was something she had always yearned for, but never got to share with her own family. She happily re-entered Tony's bedroom, and found him comfortably sleeping in bed. She picked up his clothes off the floor and the tiny jewelery box had fell out of Tony's jacket. She picked it up, and opened it, and felt breathless after having seen the sparkling and exquisite large diamond stone on the ring. She knew it was for her. She could see the words *Tony 4 Kerri* engraved around the band. She felt so excited; she had to hold back her scream. She quickly placed the ring inside the jacket, and gently slipped under the bed sheet, giving Tony a gentle kiss beside his mouth. He reacted with a smile to her kiss, and remained sleeping. And Kerri gently laid her head onto his chest, and hoped to get some sleep after having felt thrilled by what she had seen.

CHAPTER EIGHTEEN

The next morning, Tony got out of bed, and felt much revived after a good night's sleep. He stood beside the door, staring at Kerri, making breakfast for the children. He was already beginning to feel that Consuela was a long lost thing from the past.

'Papa', Fabio delightly screamed, extending his arms out to Tony.

'How are you sweetheart?' Tony said to Kerri, picking up Fabio from his seat. And they both exchanged a light kiss.

'Good, baby.' Kerri smiled.

'You know, you don't have to do this.'

'Don't be silly. You know I want to. Besides I'm very fond of both you and the kids', she rubbed Tony's shoulder, and passed Daniela her milk bottle. 'I made you some scrambled eggs.'

'I will drive you to work with me', Tony offered Kerri, as he began to have some of his breaky.

'I'm not going to work', Kerri smiled.

'Are you feeling sick or somethin'?' Tony curiously asked.

'No. No. I'm just never going to work.' Kerri put her arms around his neck from behind him.

'I don't understand.' Tony tilted his head towards her.

'What I mean. Is that. You don't have to take the kids over to your mum's. Because I'm going to always be here to look after you and the kids.'

'Are you serious? But what about your work life.'

'Shh!' she placed her index finger against his lips, 'Seriously, I don't care about work. I just want to be Mrs. Tony Abrucci.' Kerri smiled.

Tony felt ecstatic about her sacrifice and great devotion to him. He couldn't believe that another woman, beside Kerri, would give up work to look after him and the kids. He was amazed that Kerri, the modern woman, would retract to a housewife devotee.

'I love you so much, babe. Where have you been all my life?' Tony said, and gave Kerri a big long passionate kiss. 'I'm so glad to have you. I don't deserve to have such a wonderful woman in my life.' He smiled.

'And I don't deserve to have a prince in my life either.' They both exchanged smiles and small kisses, and laughed after being squirted with milk from Daniela's bottle.

'I'll grab a quick shower, and head off to work.' Tony said, as he headed off to the bathroom. He saw a picture of both Consuela and him on the window ledge. He grabbed it and threw it in the waste bin. 'Goodbye and good riddance', he said with a grin.

Fifteen minutes later, Tony came dashing down the hallway in a business suit and a briefcase. He could see that Daniela was in her pram, and Kerri was putting Fabio's hat on. 'Where are you lucky people off too?' he said with a smile, and gave Kerri a gentle kiss to the mouth.

'To the park, Papa.' Fabio excitedly commented.

'Have a good time, son. Papa has to go to work'. He kissed him on the forehead, and dashed off towards his car. They all waved good-bye to each other, as Tony took the car out of the drive way.

Half an hour later, Tony found Dina awaiting him in his office.

'What a pleasant surprise', Tony said, as they exchanged kisses.

'How are you feeling?' Dina sounded concerned.

'Well, if you're referring to Consuela. She's a thing from the past.'

'It seems that your dealing with Consuela's

abandonment pretty well. Are you sure you're not denying any feelings of hurt or neglect. Perhaps feelings of anxiety.'

'No, Sis. There's nothing for you to worry about. Actually, I couldn't be any happier.' Tony commented with a broad grin, as he soughted through a pile of papers on his desk. Dina looked at Tony very curiously, and could not help but to wonder if her brother was actually dealing too fast with his marital breakdown.

'You sure seem very happy this morning.' She moved closer towards him.

'I am. It's been a very long time since I have left the house and come to work feeling very happy, and not restless.' He could see Dina looking very puzzled at him. 'Let me fill you in on a little secret.' Tony said, as they both took a seat on the office sofa.

'Well, Sis. I'll just come out with it. Kerri and I have shared a close relationship. Well actually. We have been lovers for the past few weeks. We share a great bond, and I feel very comfortable being with her. We are very much in love with each other. And it is only a matter of time before I officially announce our engagement to the family.'

Dina was speechless. She felt totally stunned by what she had just heard.

'Well. Aren't you going to say something?' Tony said.

'I mean. I'm really happy for you. But, I never thought, you were the person for extra-marital affairs.'

'Please, Dina. Don't even begin to think about my relationship with Kerri in this way. My affair with Kerri is very genuine, and I don't believe there is anything deceitful about it. We share true love, and not just sheer passion. We have denied our true feelings of love for years now. Both Kerri and I had realized that our feelings for each other were very strong, and had

145

certainly crossed the boundaries of friendship.'

'It's just I never thought of both Kerri and you in that way.' Dina said, still coming to terms with her shock.

'Besides my marriage and love making with Consuela had ended a long time ago.' Tony stood up, feeling a bit restless about Dina taking a bit of time to give him her full blessings. 'You've got to understand that I am really in love with Kerri, and I miss every minute I'm away from her.' Tony tried to desperately convince Dina of his genuine love.

'Besides I thought you'd be happy for me, Sis.' He sighed, stroking his fingers through his hair.

'Oh! Tony I am very happy for you. I'm sorry if I seemed a little hesitant about the news. It's just that I was startled to learn about you and Kerri. Don't worry; I am very happy for you. You deserve to be happy, especially now that Consuela's gone.' She hugged him, and he gave his sister a kiss on the cheek. 'Well I can see you're in good spirits. So I better go, before my ten o'clock appointment.' Dina said, and left.

Sylvana sat under the garden gazebo, looking through family albums, reminiscing about her past with Dominic. She had still worn black clothes since her husband's burial. She clutched the crucifix in her pendant with a great sigh, as she came across a happy photo with Dominic and her. She realized that the family had not received any threatening parcels since Dominic's death. She felt that this was a strange coincidence. One of the maid's had come out to pass Sylvana the phone. Her brother Giovanni was at the other end of the line, calling from Italy. He wanted her to come with Gino to visit him. He told her that his wife had recently passed away, and with all his kids being married, he could do with the company. Giovanni had desperately missed her. It had been ten years since

Sylvana had visited family and friends back in Italy.

Giovanni convinced Sylvana to spend the next two weeks with Gino in Italy. Sylvana thought that both Gino and she could do with a break. They had both been cooped up at the estate, since Dominic's funeral. At times Gino attended daily Youth camps, but even he was bored from being glued to the internet up in his room. He whole heartedly accepted Sylvana's invitation to Italy. He felt both Sylvana and himself could do with a change in scenery. That night Gino used the internet to book two seats on the next available flight to Italy. He used his mother's credit card to confirm their departure in two days. He felt very excited and looked forward to meeting his uncle and cousins in Italy.

CHAPTER NINETEEN

Later that same week, Tony sat in his office chair staring at some business reports coming through the fax tray. It had only been three days since Sylvana and Gino had left the States to Italy, and he was already sorely missing them. He had this natural emotional tie to family and kinship. Besides his work, Tony enjoyed spending time with the family. He was looking forward to having dinner an hour later with Kerri and the kids. It was moments later that his mobile had rang, and it was Kerri at the other end of the line. She sounded very frightened and nervous.

'What? Slow down, babe. I can't hear you' Tony said.

'It's Daniela. We're at the hospital. There's something wrong with her. Please come. Hurry.' Kerri cried. Tony quietly ran out of the office, and drove fast to Craigie Children's hospital. He forgot to ask Kerri which hospital they were at, but he assumed that they would be at the children's hospital. He ran through the infantry ward and asked about Daniela at the nurses' station. The nurse had told him that she was being examined by two doctors up in theatre, and that it was best for him to wait for Dr. Millington in the patients lounge.

Tony sadly stood staring at Kerri who sat rocking in her seat, with Fabio sound asleep in her lap. She caught a glimpse of Tony at the door, and she seemed to be very distraught with tears trickling down her face. Tony could tell from her eyes that Daniela's case was a serious one. He sat beside her and kissed her on the head.

'I'm so sorry, Tony. I'm so sorry.' Kerri cried. And Tony hugged her with his eyes consumed with tears.

'What happened?' Tony asked.

'I was with Fabio watching T.V. and Daniela was having a nap. Later, I went to check up on her. Oh! It was horrible. Poor Daniela.' Kerri broke down in tears, and found it difficult to continue to speak.

'Shhh! It's all right baby. It's not your fault. Just tell me what happened.' Tony comforted her.

'She. She was all blue. She found it hard to breathe. And there was white stuff coming out of her mouth.' Kerri continued to cry.

'Shhh! It'll be all right.' Tony quietly said, with a tear strolling down his cheek. He put on a tough exterior, but deep inside he knew Daniela's case was a very serious one. Tony assumed it must be a case of SIDS. He hoped and prayed that his baby daughter wouldn't die. Forty minutes later, Tony was waltzing up and down the room, eagerly awaiting news from the doctor. Tony covered Kerri with his jacket who lay asleep next to Fabio. He had greatly appreciated Kerri's concern about his daughter. It had further reinforced the fact that Kerri had deeply cared about Tony and his children. And he was glad to have Kerri's company in this moment of ecstasy.

Twenty minutes later, Dr. Millington had approached the patients' lounge, only to find Tony staring sadly at the floor, and Kerri feeding Fabio some candy from the vending machine.

'Are you the patient's family?' She asked. And both Tony and Kerri stood up, and Tony nodded his head. They could tell from the doctor's face that things had looked very bad. Kerri's eyes were already heavily consumed with tears, and she had hoped not to hear what she thought the doctor was about to say.

'Is it a case of SIDS, doctor?' Tony asked.

'Well you could say something like that', Dr. Millington reluctantly spoke, 'We discovered a bacterial virus that had spread to over eighty per cent of

Daniela's lungs. She was critically ill on arrival, and we did all we could.' Kerri broke down in tears. 'I'm sorry. But Daniela passed away five minutes ago. I'm sorry.' The doctor quietly spoke and left. Tony's eyes were consumed with tears, and a nerve began to twitch in his upper lip. He felt greatly distressed, but he promised himself not to cry as much as he did at Dominic's funeral. But he had found it difficult to hold back some of the tears that had spurted down his face. It had only been several weeks since Dominic's funeral, and Tony was distressed to see another family member go. Kerri and Fabio hugged Tony, and they remained weeping in each other's arms for a while in the patients lounge.

Daniela was buried over the weekend, and Tony's family was deeply moved by her death. Sylvana and Gino were very upset over the news they had received from relatives back in Italy, and Sylvana could not wait to return home a week later. She helplessly yearned to be by Tony's side to comfort him during his time of grief. Sylvana could only begin to imagine what Tony must be going through, as she could not bare to lose one of her children. She had always prayed to die first before any of her children. Three days later, Tony decided to go back to work, as he could no longer stand his hallucinations of Daniela's presence in the house. He explained to Kerri that work might perhaps help him to get Daniela of his mind. Tony returned to his office, only to find a letter from Consuela on his desk. The envelope had been stamped from England.

'Dear Tony. I hope that you and the children are doing well. I'm sorry to have left you like that, but we both knew that our marriage would not last forever. You have never understood my feelings, and I badly needed a change in direction. For my sanity's sake anyway. Shaun

and I are happy together, and we're expecting our first child late April next year. I hope that you have found someone to take care of you and the children. The reason I am writing this letter is to free my conscious from guilt. I thought that it was only fair to tell you that Daniela is not really your daughter. She was conceived after Nunzio and I had made passionate love one afternoon. It was only that afternoon, Nunzio came over with a bottle of champagne, we got drunk, spilling out our life sorrows to each other, and one thing had led to another. I really did not want to cheat on you, but I was drunk, and had been neglected from passionate love for a long time. I'm sorry. I hope you will forgive me. Consuela'.

Tony was boiling mad from Consuela and scrunched up the letter, and threw it hard across the room. He would have loved to be close to Consuela to throttle her neck. He thought she was a real bitch to keep something as important as this from him. On top of things, she had made him grieve for a little girl that wasn't even his. Tony felt even angrier by the fact that Consuela was insinuating that it was his fault for her rendez vous with Nunzio. He grabbed his keys and felt like going over to the cottage to punch the living daylights out of Nunzio, when suddenly he caught a glimpse of a strange fax coming through his tray that had looked like a photo of a group of people. His office phone began to ring, and Tony stared at it for a moment, and then decided to answer it. It turned out to be the private investigator, Tony had hired, calling from Italy.

'Hello! Tony. It's Vincent.'

'Vincent. What's up?' Tony sounded very curious.

'Well! I hope you're ready for this. I have some

important information to tell you.'

'Shoot Vinnie. I'm all ears.'

'Well! It seems that your brother-in-law is not really who he seems to be.'

'I don't understand. By the way is the fax I'm about to receive from you.'

'Yes. I just faxed it. It's a photo of Fabruzio. Or should I say Nunzio and his father. Apparently Nunzio's real name is Fabruzio Corsini. He is the son of a well known mafia leader, Antonio Corsini. Corsini was a big time gangster decades ago in Sicily. He was the leader of a group called Black Scorpion.'

'Oh! My God. Papa knew Antonio and members of Black Scorpion.' Tony was very shocked to learn the truth about Nunzio, and the fact that Nunzio's family had something to do with his father's past.

'Well! If you take a closer look at the newspaper article I have faxed you, you will see a photo of his deceased father. Now you may not be able to read the Italian print well, but apparently it says that Fabruzio. Well Nunzio. He has solemnly sworn to avenge his father's killer. It says something about Nunzio going to U.S.A. to track down a dishonoured member of the Black Scorpion.' Tony's eyes were wide open with great horror. Tony knew that the dishonoured member of the group had to have been his father. He began to feel very frightened for the safety of his sister Dina.

'Are you there, Tony?' Vincent asked.

'Yes. Yes. I'm here. Thanks a lot for everything Vinnie.'

'Well I guess I'll see you in L.A. in a couple of days.'

'Okay! Vinnie. Great work. Ciao.' Tony put down the telephone receiver. He took a few moments, staring at Nunzio in the faxed photograph. He felt outraged by Nunzio's deception of the family. It had explained a lot of the family problems that the Abrucci's had gone through in the past few years. 'You son of a bitch, Nunz. The game is over.' Tony commented as he scrunched the fax and placed it in his jacket's pocket. He grabbed his mobile, and dialed the cottage. The phone kept ringing, but no one was picking up at the other end.

'C'mon Dina. C'mon Sis. Pick up the damn phone.' Tony anxiously spoke to himself.

CHAPTER TWENTY

Dina could hear the phone ringing from outside the cottage, as she was experiencing some difficulty in managing to remove the last grocery bag out of her car. And by the time she had used the keys to open the front door, and settle the grocery bags onto the kitchen table, the phone had stopped ringing. She noticed through the kitchen window Nunzio doing some carpentry work on the green house in the back garden. She found it strange to see Nunzio working for the first time out in the cottage's garden. He usually spent his work leave hanging with friends down China town. She didn't think anything of it, and went into the study to arrange an appointment with the best gynecologist in California. During the past year, Dina had been desperately trying to fall pregnant, as she had always wanted a child of her own. She had been earlier to see Dr. Wilkinson at the mall's clinic, who had given her a referral to see a specialist.

Tony had tried to call Dina on her mobile, but he had only managed to reach her voicemail. 'Damn it', Tony yelled, as he slammed his mobile hard against his desk. Dina had earlier switch off her mobile when she visited the mall's clinic, and had forgotten to turn it back on again. Tony grabbed his car keys and mobile, and hurriedly went to his car. He had been using Kerri's Renault that day, because the Corvette was low on petrol. He decided to drive down to Bel Air to Dina's cottage. Tony retried calling Dina at the cottage. And Dina was aware of an incoming call to the cottage, as she was making her appointment. She answered it, and Tony was glad he had reached her at last.

'At last, Sis. I have been trying to call you.' Tony sounded a little nervous.

'Is everything all right?' Dina worriedly asked. She

could tell there was something wrong from the sound in Tony's voice.

'I'm on my way to the Cottage. Sit tight until I arrive.' Tony's mobile started to make a sound, indicating that he had a very low battery. And Tony felt very frightened off losing his sister over the line.

'Listen I have a low battery. Nunzio is not who he seems to be. He's a very dangerous man. Do not aggravate him in anyway.' Tony hurriedly spoke to her.

'Can you hear me, Sis?' There began to be an interference with the line, and they both experienced some difficulty in hearing each other.

'Nunzio is a dangerous man. Stay put I'm coming.' Tony screamed into his mobile phone.

'What do you mean?' Dina was shocked to hear him say that her husband was a dangerous man, and she had hoped he would explain to her more about what he had exactly meant.

'I'll explain things when...' Tony ceased to speak, realizing that he had lost total contact with his sister.

'What do you mean dangerous? Hello. Hello. Tony. Are you still there?' Dina had also realized that the line between them had been disconnected. Tony angrily threw his mobile onto the front passenger's seat. And put his foot down hard onto the accelerator and began to dodge some of the cars ahead of him at full speed. He had hoped that Dina would not confront Nunzio about their conversation over the phone.

Dina began to feel somewhat suspicious of Tony's call, and she wondered what he had meant about Nunzio being dangerous. She gazed through the study's window, and she could see that Nunzio was busy engaged with working on the green house. She went to place her gynecologist's referral into the drawer, and was startled to find a lot receipts from the Le Marina Sea fresh store down by the Californian Bay. And she

155

was more shocked to learn that Nunzio had spent a lot of money purchasing fresh scorpions. She looked out the window again with wide open eyes, where Nunzio remained busy making amendments to the glass green house.

Dina decided to run upstairs to their bedroom to look for Nunzio's secret box. She shuffled through the bedroom drawer, pulling out some under garments, and threw them onto the floor. She then checked the bedside cabinets, and felt frustrated about not locating the secret box there. She then savagely roamed through their wardrobes, and later pulled the dressing table stool to reach the top wardrobe shelf. She had removed some hat and shoe boxes onto the ground, and she had extended her arm further towards the back, grabbing a hold of Nunzio's small safety box. She could see there was a tiny lock on it. She threw the box onto the bed, and ran downstairs to grab a chisel from the laundry, and later returned to the bedroom. Dina sat frustrated as she found it difficult to break through the tiny lock. She angrily began to hit the box against the mahogany bed post, and a couple of tears had trickled down the side of her cheeks. She later used the thick chisel to bang it hard against the lock's latch, and was surprised to see that the latch had broken off with the lock still securely attached to it. She slowly lifted the top metal lid of the box, and was shocked to see a number of Italian newspaper articles, some photographs, a broche, and a gold watch.

Dina was very shocked to see a picture of Nunzio with his parents. He had always told the family that he grew up in a Sicilian orphanage. And she was even more shocked to learn that Nunzio's real name was Fabruzio Corsini, and she had come across an old newspaper clipping which indicated that Antonio Corsini, the leader of Black Scorpion mafia was found dead in a mineshaft. Dina's eyes were wide open with horror. She could see that Antonio was the same person in Nunzio's family photo. She had also seen the name Antonio Corsini engraved at the back of the gold watch.

'Oh! My God. Antonio is Nunzio's father.' She quickly placed all of Nunzio's belonging back into the box, and used the bed post to lift herself off the ground.

Dina grabbed the lock and latch and also placed them into the box, and returned it back into the wardrobe. She hurriedly threw some of their clothes and boxes into the wardrobe, and as she closed the wardrobe, she caught a mirror reflection of Nunzio at the door. Dina screamed with great fright, and quickly turned around. Nunzio stood silently leaning against the door in a black chesty singlet, jeans and garden boots, with a strap of shed tools around his waist.

'You gave me quite a scare. I was just tiding some of our clothes.' Dina nervously said, as she pretended to fold one of her neck scarves on the bed. She began to feel very frightened and her hands began to slightly tremble, as Nunzio continued to silently stare at her from the door way.

'So how's the green house coming along?' She nervously spoke, avoiding eye contact with him.

'You should have never opened it.' Nunzio coldly said.

'What do you mean?' Dina tried to act naïve, but she knew he was well onto her about opening his secret box.

'You should have never opened it, damn it.' Nunzio screamed, bashing his fist against the door. And Dina shook with great fright.

'You're responsible for Papa's death, weren't you Fabruzio?' Dina snapped at him, and her eyes were heavily consumed with tears. 'Why? Why did you do it,

157

Nunzio?' she said.

'Well! Inspector Abrucci has finally put the missing jigsaw together.' Nunzio said, as he slowly walked around her. 'Why? Because I fricken hate you all. Especially you and your father. Your father killed my father. Now that's not fair, is it, Ballerina.' He screamed from behind her with great rage. And Dina stood silently staring across the room with tears trickling down her face.

'Now I'm the black scorpion, and you're my final sting.' Nunzio said.

Dina ran towards the door, but Nunzio was quick in stopping her, grabbing a hold of her arm and hair. He slapped her hard across the face, and began to furiously strangle her. She was having difficulty in releasing herself from his tight grip, and she was beginning to slowly suffocate. She reached for the hammer in his waist belt and used it to hit him hard on the side of his head. Nunzio screamed from excruciating pain, letting her go free, clutching his head with both hands. Dina desperately gasped for air holding onto her throat with one hand, and used the other to help pick her up off the ground. She quickly ran downstairs, and out the front door, towards her car. She realized that she had left her keys on the kitchen table with the other grocery bags. And she could see from outside Nunzio coming down the stairs with one hand glued to his head.

Dina decided to run across to her old widow neighbour, Mrs. Henreich. She knocked heavily on her door. 'Mrs. Henreich. Mrs. Henreich. Please open the door. I need you to help me.' She cried for help. She could see Nunzio shuffling his feet coming across the road towards her. Dina desperately continued to knock on Mrs. Henreich's door, hoping that she would soon open it. When Nunzio was getting closer to Dina's side, she decided to run through the side gate and into the garden. She hid behind the outdoor barbeque. Nunzio kicked the side gate open, and entered Mrs. Henreich's garden. He gazed across the garden but he could not see Dina anywhere.

'Dina. Dina. Come out. I know you're hiding. I just want to talk to you.' Nunzio shouted. He moved up closer towards the barbeque area and the swimming pool. 'Come out, ballerina', he screamed.

Dina remained sitting tight behind the barbeque area, trembling with fear. She decided to run further across the back lawn, but Nunzio had run extra fast from behind her and threw himself onto her, and they both made a big splash into the swimming pool. Nunzio swam up to her, grabbing her by the hair, as Dina released some water from her mouth and gasped for air. Nunzio kept putting her head under the water and later pulled her head from underneath the water, as Dina frantically gasped for air. 'How do you like that, Dina? Tell me. How do you like that?' Nunzio angrily spoke to her.

Tony had pulled his car outside the cottage, and he was shocked to see the front door open, and tiny blood spots on the ground. He slowly made his way across the road as he followed the trail of blood spots over to Mrs. Henreich's front gate. Dina screamed loud, as Nunzio pulled her close to him, and locked his full hand onto her throat. Tony heard her cry from the front garden, and ran towards the open side garden gate. Nunzio lifted out a large razor blade tool from his waist belt, and he had every intention of harming Dina with it.

'Fabruzio', Tony screamed, as he stood shocked beside the garden barbeque. And Nunzio had glanced towards him. Tony's presence had taken him by surprise. 'Don't you dare, Fabruzio. You have already caused a great deal of damage to this family.' Tony sounded very threatening. And Nunzio just stared at him with a grin.

Dina took the opportunity of Tony's interruption to knee Nunzio in the groin, and began to swim fast towards her brother, leaving Nunzio behind in excruciating pain.

'Hurry, Sis. Swim faster.' Tony yelled out to Dina, stretching out his hand, whilst grabbing a hold of the side pool lamp.' Nunzio had noticed Tony pull Dina out of the pool, and his eyes grew wide open, as he was shocked to see that the huge outdoor lamp was attached to a long cord connected all the way across to the external garden power point. He quickly attempted to swim towards the side of the pool, but Tony had thrown the lamp into the water, electrocuting Nunzio whilst inside it. Nunzio's body aggravatedly shook in the water, and Dina burrowed her face into her brother's shoulder, as she could not stand watching Nunzio's agony. Tony shockingly looked towards Nunzio, as Nunzio's eyes remained wide open and his body floated on the surface of the water.

'It's all right, Sis. You're safe now.' Tony said, placing his suit jacket around her shoulders. Dina continued to silently weep as Tony gently escorted her across the garden.

CHAPTER TWENTY ONE

A year later, the Abrucci family was beginning to move on with their own lives. Sylvana was upstairs with the family doctor who was probing Gino's knees with a metal instrument. There was a new drug being trialed in the medical market for quadriplegics, and the family doctor had convinced Gino to participate in the experiment with little hope that Gino might walk again. Sylvana and Gino had discussed this new form of drug therapy, and they thought it was worth a try without having high hopes on the matter. Besides Gino thought he had nothing to lose, since he was bound to a wheelchair for the rest of his life. The doctor pulled up the doona to cover Gino's legs.

'What's the prognosis, doctor?' Sylvana asked. She had promised herself not to get emotionally bound to a medical experiment that may later lead to false promises.

'Well Sylvana. I have to be honest with you. There is yet to be any startling change since day one of the experiment. I'm seeing little response in Gino's reflexive actions to some of the general probing. So it's still worthwhile for Gino to continue to visit our medical lab next week. Besides the drug seems to be eliminating some of the pain Gino experiences from osteoporoses.'

Dina entered the bedroom with two espressos and a creamy café latte for Gino. Dina had sold the cottage, opened her own private counseling practice in Beverly Hills, and had moved back into the estate with Sylvana and Gino.

'How are you doing, Champ?' Dina asked Gino, passing him his cup. And Sylvana and the doctor left the room.

'Oh! The doctor just says that the drug seems to be

helping with the pain in my knees.'

'Well. It's better than nothing, aye kiddo'. Dina smiled. 'Are you coming down later for dinner?'

'Yeap!' Gino nodded.

Tony came down the stairs, and used the hallway grand mirror to form a knot in his tie, while Kerri and Fabio were putting on their coats at the front door.

'Papa, Papa. Are we going to nanas?' Fabio excitedly asked.

'We sure are champ.' Tony said, lifting him up in his arms, giving him a great bear hug and a kiss. 'How are you feeling babe?' Tony turned to Kerri. He had referred to Kerri being pregnant, as her stomach was already showing.

'I'm okay, besides minor migraines. I'll be fine.' Kerri smiled.

'You know, this is our first official family dinner as husband and wife.'

'So it is.'

'I can't believe we're actually married. So do you think you can keep up with the Abrucci's melodramas?'

'I'll try to make sacrifices, here and there, to keep going', Kerri smiled. They both laughed, and exchanged two light kisses to the mouth before leaving the house.

Dina noticed her mother going through some family airlooms, after having left Gino's room. 'Strolling down memory lane, I see Mama.' Dina stood at the door smiling.

'Just looking at some sentimental things. They bring back memories from the past. You know, some of these things are precious antiques.' Sylvana held up an exquisite old antique pendant in her hand. 'You know, this has been passed down, generations. My great, great grandmother used to own this beautiful pendant.'

162

'It sure is a beautiful antique.' Dina commented moving in closer to her mother.

'I want you to have it, Ballerina.'

'Oh! Are you sure Mama? It's very extravagant.'

'Oh! Yes. I'm very sure. This pendant has been passed down from mother to daughter. And I would like you to cherish it with the fondest memories.'

'I will Mama. Thank you.' Their eyes were overwhelmed with joyful tears. Dina hugged her mother. They could hear Thea calling them from downstairs, informing them that Tony and his family had arrived.

Sylvana sat at the head of the table with a grin. Tonight was a special family dinner organized by Dina to celebrate Kerri's pregnancy. She had fallen pregnant for the first time in her life, since marrying Tony four months ago. Tony and Kerri were happily married, and they had bought a small mansion in Beverly Hills closer to the family estate. Fabio was seated happily beside his father, nibbling at his small dinner plate. On the other side of the table sat Nicole in between Dina, who carried one of the twins, and Gino, who fed the other her milk bottle.

'So I hear you're expecting a baby boy.' Sylvana talked to Kerri.

'Yes. I had my ultrasound done yesterday.'

'Congratulations darling.'

'Thank you, Sylvana.'

'So what are you thinking of naming your son?' Sylvana asked her.

'Dominic, of course.' Kerri said with no hesitation. And Tony looked very pleased with Kerri. They had never discussed any names for the baby. He was very surprised to learn that Kerri was thinking of naming their son after his father. But then again, he knew Kerri was always a bright woman, and always had the right words to say. He loved her a lot for her genuine loyalty for him and the family. Tony put his arm around Kerri, and gave her a gentle kiss to the mouth.

Sylvana looked around the table with a broad grin. She was glad to see the family happily reunited over another special dinner. But deep inside her heart she had yearned for Joey's presence. She had missed her son a great deal, and she sadly awaited his release which was due four months later. She proposed a toast for Joey's safe return, and the whole family raised their wine goblets in hope and prosperity.

THE END